What Is It Press Copyright 2018
Editor: Sebastian De Angelis
Author: Sue Yan Nish
Series Start Date: 11-26-2013
Revised: 03-24-2020
ISBN: 978-0-9679947-4-1
ASIN: B07D5K478Z
GGKEY: 6W6WKEFDDGN E

Publishers Note: although some references to historical events may be made throughout this book, the content is fictional and intended for adult readers only.

The manual (SM069) is no longer provided in the appendix of the books in the Empty Nation (EN) series because it grew beyond a reasonable size. So it's published separately on Amazon (small cost), Google Play Books (free) and also available for free when you purchase this title on Audible.com, the accompanying PDF support material (SM069) will be available in your Audible Library along with the audio book.

References to Manual are made throughout the books in the series. Tag format: the word being referenced is tagged in **bold** print preceding the reference in square brackets. Reference format: a period [**.**] the dot symbol is used to separate the components of the reference, as in the following examples.

Tag [*section* dot *sub-section* dot *description*]

SIT [4.D-G2.22], section 4, sub-section D-G2, description 22
PBS [2.10], section 2, description 10
SEC [26], section 26

EN03: the Truth

C01 College Part A: The Gurls, or whatever you want to refer to them as at this point in the series, livestock, genetic mutations, hermaphrodites, sex-toys, test-tube babies, are in their first year of college. Their education includes how to shower with the boys, the epic literary work called the Rise and Fall of the American Penis (RFAP), Sissyology class. As naive freshmen they're recruited for the NSA and make marriage plans. Ahh… College! Jane is put under Professor Yaoi's spell.

C02 College Part B: Studbucks©, Sex Psychology 101. In the year 2251 gay-sex, of course, is illegal in the USA Inc. with the exception of Man-on-Man sex, or MOM [4.D-G4.19] sex which is permitted only to wealthy high-ranking Stud class men for research and therapeutic proposes. Professor Rimme puts Mary under her spell. The Gurls learn about the Homo-Femininus (FEM) who turns Sissy-Gurls into sex-slaves with their psychotropic love-cream. Whorehouse® duties in their dorm, at an NSA meeting the Gurls are sedated with magic, jizzed-up, tea by the Professors.

C03 Inoculation: Unbeknownst to the Gurls they are being groomed for a completely new mission in life. They're seduced, prepared, indoctrinated & branded into Pimp Whore Partnerships (**PWP**) in affiliation with the USA Inc. Department of Commerce and the Church, the HCC. After they're returned to the dorm the Gurls are shocked to discover millions in their bank accounts. Shockingly they discover both of them have had their Vaganus® turned into Rosebuds (permanently prolapsed) and ass cheeks branded with their Pimps (Rimme & Yaoi) serial number.

C04 the Truth: Mary & Jane are startled at first of their new prestigious positions (Pimp owned Nuns) in a religious cult orgasmization (HCC). But they cum to the realization, life in the new America ain't as awful as they thought. After a wild and secret escapade for the church, they take their vows of promiscuity and be cum Nuns in a harem. Then finally, although skeptical about the government's scheme to use sex as a cum-modity, they accept the new **truth**. After all, their Pimps were offering the Gurls a new and wonderful life full of adventure with the chances to achieve world-peace by reducing human violence though sexual pleasure. And to a couple of carefree Homo-Sis-Sapien, Bonobo-Love® type Gurls nothing could be more desirable.

Books in the Empty Nation (EN) Series

EN02: Growing-Up

C01 Sissy preschool: This is book 2 of the Empty Nation series. The Gurls (Mary & Jane) are simply man-handled and playfully abused by Stud® class men. They've trained to perform Sissy-Love®. Starting from preschool, these young adorable Gurls engage in promiscuous, lewd if human, noting here, the Sissy, although not naturally occurring on earth are still registered as livestock animals in the USA Inc. Other Sissydom issues are, the Pledge of Allegiance, humiliation training the **Piss-On-Me** ritual, social class Opt-Out®, Jane is reprimanded for being naughty.

C02 JAS Camp: The mom's scheme about creating a perfect DOM-Bitch Bonded Pair, a **DBBP®**. The Gurls survive Scout camp unharmed. They're satisfied emotionally and physically. And are exposed to many intimate situations with camp (vacation resort) guests as they grow-up in the new USA Inc. Junior American Sissy camp is just what the Gurls need to feel liberated from their overly loving parents. Discuss, government supplied Sissy-Breeding® **D** and **B formulas** and the Mind Control **MCD** drugs, Pool-Party, Snowballing, Bonobo-Love®.

C03 Elementary School: The story in the series is further defined by boring lectures about **Sissydom®** from elementary school teachers. Every class filled with ramblings on about USA Inc. propaganda and dollar hegemony. Knowledge of the new Whore-for-Profit® world in the Modern Social Economic System, **MSES®** is brainwashed into the innocent Gurls®. Also reviewed in this chapter are, Hono-Sis-Sapien®, Sex gym class, modern history, sociology, Labor Compensation Transaction, **LCT®**.

C04 High School: The Gurls are taught the MSES® is a newly created system of governance which rewards sexual prowess where size matters. Free love, free sex! And the downtrodden citizenry is quite pleased despite most of the population living in FEMA zones (little do they know, in the camps, senior citizens are ground-up into food products). An even more sick & twisted change is, society in the future has again accepted a class system. The new system promotes men who are wealthy and so can afford penis enlargement drugs **PED**®. This Stud® class is sexually well-endowed and abuses citizens based on their mediocre sexual ability. Also reviewed and referenced, American Economic Disparity, the **AED**®, Penis Official Length Certificate, **POLC**®, Sissy gang violence of transmutation, **TM**®, one unit of money is equal to one unit of a male-orgasm, a **MO**®.

Books in the Empty Nation (EN) Series

Empty Nation

A dirty story about a dirty country

Series (1), Book (3)

The Truth

Sue Yan Nish

Table of Contents

Chapter: 1 College Part A

The year is 2251...

[1.1] ARRIVING

Mary here it is, room 069, this is our room.

Okay, I'll swipe the keycard. Wow! Mary exclaims). Jane, its sooo big!

Ooooh yeah, well, it's a full Sissy-suite not just a dorm-room, Unfucking-believable. Look at all the mirrors on the walls and ceiling. Awesome! I love it!

Jane, it's because the folks here at the Federal University of Cultural Integration Transition, the **FUCIT** [3.C1.4] know us Sissy® Gurls need all the amenities of a Whorehouse® while we're here at an Integration College.

Mary let's just drop our stuff off and go look around campus for some boys. Mwah...

Sure, **Jane** you want to go prowling, but don't you want a douche-out first? My lovehole is leaking all over the place. I took a lot of loads on the train.

Hmmm... I especially liked the part when we were making-out while they screwed us. Mwah... (Jane drapes her tiny little body over Mary). Mwah... I always wanna be holding you when I got a Dude in me. I can't believe it, we're finally here! We're in College! Mwah...

Yeah me too Lover. Kiss... It was one big college fuckfest on the way here with all those Stud students on the train. Wooo… I'm tired (Mary the DOM has about half the energy as a Bitch-Type like Jane does).

Ummm… But can we first just go walking around? Please **Mare**? I feel super sexy with cum all over my body. And you know me, I like cum flowing down my leg. I don't care how cum drench my sexy school girl knee-high socks get! Mwah…

Oooh Jane! Okay Lover, let's check out the campus real quick. Mwah…

Mwah... Thanks Babe!

[1.2] CAMPUS

Yeah Jane, I know you Gurlfriend. Kiss... kisssss... You like the filled-up feeling. Huh okay! (Mary sighs). Let's check-out the FUCIT campus.

Thanks! Mwah… Besides Mary, I think the smell of sperm from my thoroughly worked cunt attracts Stud® boys to me. All those Sissy pheromones mixed with Man-Cream.

Jane, this would account for you having the highest **Cockage**® total in our high school. Geeezz… Jane, I can't believe you're Sexual Activity Rating. Your **SAR** [5] is **Wild Flower** with, 100,000 Sissy penetrations. Jane like I always say, you're a cock-magnet!

Well Gurlfriend I definitely have a system! (Jane says in a matter of fact tone).

Oooh! Really Jane? Tell me you Hoe, how do you score so high?

Sure I'll tell you, but only because you're my Bff. Hmm... Kisss.

Mwah... Professor Jane, please continue. Hmm...

Well, when a Stud smells a Sissy-in-Heat and she has cum oozing out of her freshly screwed Vaganus®, Studs naturally desire the Sissy®. And even more so if she's carrying around between her sexy legs a big ball of Jizz in her Clit-Sock®, straining her poor little clit. Now that's what American Stud boys want!

Wow! Jane, you just desired a Hoe! You sure this is scientific?

Of course I am. Mwah... Heee hee... They wanna a Sissy Gurl® who has been taken advantage of. If she has all the signs she's been very sexually active, she's a total turn-on! Even though the smell of Man-Cream, aka human Dick-Milk, has a negligible hallucinogenic effect. The Sissy-Cream on the other hand absolutely does. You can check the effects from the Cream or Poop Severity, **COPS** [18.13] data in the Sissydom® manual.

Seriously **Jane**, you're gonna start talking about the technical issues associated with Dick-Milk?

Mare! No! You know I don't care about Sissy-Science crap! What I'm saying is, sexually speaking its better if the sperm is dripping down a Gurls leg. Call it a, mood setting effect.

Wow **Jane**! Haaa haa... ha... You realize you're a Slut right?

Yeah! Mare, I'm not ashamed of my sexual desires. Besides, if the Sissy® is breaking all the rules by playing with her Gurly clit and tits in public, squirting her cock-arousal pheromone all over the place, it's even hotter! It's all part of be cuming a professional Sissy-Whore®. And let's face it Mare, it turns men on! Heck! Sissy-Sex is the number one national pastime sport in the USA now! And I think copulating with a Sissy should be an Olympics event!

Wow! **Jane**, where did you read this in your Sissyology textbook?

Yeah, actually I did! But just the part about the professional Sissy stuff. The softball size Cum-Sock® dangling from a clit is my own personal observation. You know me. I'm always walking around with a Cum-Ball hanging.

Oooh yeah! You always do Gurlfriend? My precious Wildflower Sissy Gurl. Mwah… Ahhh… **Jane**, you hot little Bitch. Mwah… Mwah…

Ooooh Yeah! Kiss me Babe... Hmmm... Kiss, (Jane & Mary embrace passionately and make-out), Kissss... Oooh! I'm so happy you're my Bitch Jane... Hmm... Kiss.... I love you sooo much Jane. Mwah… Mwah…

I love you too **Mare**, Hmm.... Kisss. Aaagh! I'm squirting! I want to be married to you Babe. You know Sissies can get married to each other now when they turn eighteen.

Yes we can get Sissy-Married, but we'll still be assigned a human Sissy-Breeder Lady to be married to for breeding. Mwah…

Why Mare?

It's just the system my friend. All Sissies are assigned a breeding human female to produce Sissy babies. The Sissydom® Manual SM069 [6] thoroughly explains it.

And the new laws let Sissies be dual married, a Sissy-Marriage and also a Sissy-Breeding-Marriage (SBM). Look it up [6.E].

Yes thank you, miss know-it-all. Geeeez **Mary** why don't you run for Cunt-gress, you know all the laws. They let Sissies run for the United States House of Representatives and the Senate now?

Maybe I will Sugar-Puss. **Jane** I've always been elected a leader, Sissy Scout-Master, class president of every class. And I know I'll be elected Freshmen Class President here at FUCIT. Besides I'm so worthy of being elected with my natural ability to allure and seduce votes given my perfect human form.

Wow! Huh! You sound a little braggadocious! But yeah! **Mary** you do have a Barbie doll **DOM**® [1.A2.1] Sissy body. And Sissies easily win in political elections. I mean humans don't have half the sex appeal as a pure breed Sissy, **PBS** does.

Yep! Sex wins elections.

Oooh **Mary**! You'd win for sure and I'll be your political Whore and use my body to sway the voters for you, kissss, kiss, Mwah...

[1.3] BOYS

Prowling for Boys on campus...

Wheet Whooo! Hey beautiful? Hey Gurls? What's up? (Handsome college guy whistling at **Jane** & **Mary** on the campus quad).

Hey! Just hanging out what are you Boys up too?

Hanging out watching lesbian Sissies making-out!

Oh yeah! Mary and I put on quite a show don't we Lover?

Hmmm... Kisss.... You know it Jane. Mwah... Hmmm...

Hey I'm Jane, (Jane reaches out and does a cock-shake with the big strong college dudes prick which is obviously aroused by the huge bulge in his pants), how's it hanging? Mwah...

Well, I'm hanging a little cramped in there if you know what I mean? Mwah...

Yes, we're fully aware of you and your friends having discomfort wearing those man pants especially when you all have such huge, ragging hardons for us Sissy Gurls!

Wow! What are you suggesting? We already know you bitches are in heat, just by the cummy smell of your obviously used Sissy cunts.

Well, my friend, you're right we just got off a train and guess what? We screwed everyone on it! Here I'll prove it! (Jane reaches between her legs, scooping up a wad from her sloppy cum dripping lovehole, then brings it up to her mouth and licks it off her hand).

Hoe! Ooooh! Really? Oooh! Wow! Fuck-me!

Yeah, I will! So, why don't you and your gang of obviously horny, well hung, Stud® friends, help us test-out our new dorm-suite Whorehouse (WH)? This way my Classy Sissy DOM Mary and I can perform our whoring obligations while here at college.

Sure, sure, sure... Let's go play Boys! (All twenty of the Studs follow Mary and Jane back to the dorm WH).

The next day...

Oh okay, now I think I wanna douching! Wow! I'm too tired I can't move **Mare**.

Ahhhh… My sore cunt!

What time is it, **Mare**?

It's two in the afternoon Jane.

What happened? (Jane is holding her head).

Well, we graduated high school and then went to college.

Ha... ha...Very funny. Yep! This is college, we invited a few guys into our dorm-suite for a little afternoon delight and the next thing we know the entire football team, marching band and the ROTC unit, is banging us. I feel like I'm back at **JAS Camp** [16] after an **FO**® [7.6].

Mary Honey! The only difference is this FO, might last for the entire four years of college!

Ah! My cunts sore and my pussy lips are red! My bed and my body are drenched in cum. I think we seriously need a shower.

Mine too Lover. Yeah, let's get cleaned-up.

Mary do you still love me?

Jane, why wouldn't I?

Because I invited them into our place without your permission?

Honey-Bunny, I love you forever no matter what happens. Well, in-that-case Mary, Let's go douche and shower in the boys shower room?

Whoa! Jane Honey. The pounding you got last night wasn't enough? Anyway, we have our own gang-shower here in our super deluxe dorm Whorehouse® suite? Oh wait, I get it. Dah! You need more boys?

Yep!

You naughty little nympho! You want to shower with boys of course.

Yes Mary, you know I'm a **Type-B** [1.A2.2]. I was bio-engineered to screw men and swallow sperm. I need more than a DOM® type Sissy like you.

Yeah I get it. We have a fancy gang shower with no gang in it. **Jane** you mutant, you're ad-Dick-ted to sex!

Yeah I know I'm a Cumoholic! Or is it Cockolicism? Haa ha... Not to be confused with the defunct and replace **Catholicism** [9.A.0].

Yeah **Jane** a real cumologist ha... haa... haaa. But hey you're right Jane, what good is our beautiful deluxe shower without boys in it? Kiss... Mwah…

Wait! Cum here Honey! Look, our deluxe shower has glory holes in it.

Wow Mary! It must be adjoined to the boy's shower room? Cool Sissy Suite! They thought of everything a horny Sissy would need!

Oh check this out, I don't believe it! Here's the instruction booklet for the glory-holes, Whore House Glory-Hole **WHGH** [22.32] usage manual. Geeezzz! They did think of everything. Listen to this.

Step 1: turn red availability notice light on. This light is in the Stud shower-room. When the light is on it is red, and is a signal there is a Sissy on the Whore House side of the glory hole wall which is willing to engage in sex with a Stud participant.

Step 2: The Male Stud® may turn on the penetration hole selection light to indicate which of the Sissies two holes he wishes to engage in sex with.

Step 3: When Sissy is no longer available for said sex the Sissy needs to turn the red availability light off.

Step 4: If sexual desires persist, repeat steps 1, 2 and 3.

Well Mare it's cute and everything and hey I might be just a Type-B Sissy, but I'm not a Dumpie, I don't hear or see any dicks on the other side of this glory-hole wall. So let's just go to the Stud shower. Mwah...

Jane you got a point there smarty pants. Let's go, I desperately need a shower. And you, well we know what you need. Mwah...

[1.4] RFAP

The Gurls in the Boys Shower room...

Mary can you do my back for me Honey? Mwah...

Mwah... Sure Babe.

Oooh it feels sooo good! And the hot water on my face. Aaaah… Kissss… And these lower shower heads spraying on my thoroughly rimmed-out sore hole. Hmmm...

You have really nice tits Babe. They're so huge! (Jane is massaging Mary huge tits). Mwah…

Mwah… Thank you Honey Bunny. I do have a nice set don't I? Why didn't your parents want you to get big ones like me when you turned thirteen?

It was me.

What? You didn't want big tits? Geeeez Jane! Why NOT? I love my big lactating tits and guys do too!

I just wanted to stay small. I have a very petite little Bitch® frame and at four feet tall, the big boobs wouldn't have looked proportionally correct on me. At my height, I'd be dragging them on the floor. Hell! Maybe even trip over them! Heeee... heee... hee....

Hmm… You might! And yeah, Bitch® types are all flat. DOMs on the other hand were created with large beasts.

Oh yeah! Mare you have always had a nice ass, wide hips, tall enough at five feet and nice broad shoulders. Mary, your 48DD jugs look great on you! Honey you're a super-hot DOM Lady.

Thank you Babe. Mwah… Yeah but Jane, you're eighteen and still wear a training bra!

Yeah so what? Mary, like most other B-Types, I like having a little boy look and I love exposing my nipples in a cup-less **SissyWear**® kiddy bra. It makes me feel sexy. Beside Mary guys don't seem to mind I'm flat-chested. In fact petite little boyish prepubescent looking Sissies like me turn American men on. I wanna maintain the boyish trap look.

Well sure Jane. And yeah, what can you say? American men are perverted pedophiles for sure. They're just a product of society. But in the new Cunt-Stitution twenty-ninth **Amendment** [17.29] states, men have the constitutional right to do a Sissy up their government owned **Vaganus**® [14.O1.6], it's all part of the **MSES**. Although humans still call a Vaganus a shithole!

Mare, you know Humans ain't too bright?

Yeah! This only proves, humans are mentally challenged. They don't understand the **Homo-Sis-Sapien** [18] genome was engineered to be a sexually superior species and we have both a vagina and anal cavity in one hole, the only thing missing is a fully functional uterus.

Dah! And yeah, I agree, humans are stupid, especially the men. Sissies out score humans on IQ tests every time. And **Mare**, we both know humans are dumb, but whatever they say about Americans in other countries in regards to how immoral we are here in the United States Inc. it doesn't matter to me.

Well yeah **Jane**, the whole world knows the Imperialistic USA Inc. government is run by an Oligarchical of wealthy, not so smart aristocrats. But the American culture is just a bunch of decent normal people. And Expats were smart enough to get out of this Cunt-trie!

Yeah but **Mare**, you gotta admit. Without girly cloths on, I do look a lot like a little boy with long blonde hair.

Yeah sure! Jane, you're a really cute, hot looking Gurly Boy. Mwah… (Jane is admired for her sweet, youthful, feminine appearance). Mwah… You're Adorable. Mwah…

Thanks **Mare**. Mwah… But hey! I know I'm really a Gurl on the inside regardless of how many American men think they're screwing a little-boy in his ass when they do me. That's their problem not mine!

Well **Jane** I totally agree with you and aside from all of that, studies done by Hardon-Vard University have proven the American male is perverted. And love sticking their dicks up a little-boys ass.

Huh! Bunch of perverts!

The defense of the American male…

Ah huh! This is why they get off on doing sweet little Sissy princesses like you **Jane**. The study shows how the American male sexual desire to screw little boys in the ass, stems from a Freudian analysis where, the American male had and still does feel abandoned by the once insolvent and Plutocratic US Government which he perceives as his mother.

Mare, was this known as the American Oedipus complex? The **AOC** [23.15a] which started to manifest over the last couple of centuries. The AOC started around the 2008 financial crisis. It's all in the textbook, **The Rise & Fall of the American Penis** [21.1], the RFAP.

Yeah **Jane**, your cousin Seymour authored the RFAP.

Yeah Seymour my horny cousin wrote it. Huh! He likes calling it the FAP. Otherwise known as, fap or Master-Baiting. He said it accurately describes the book in a more explicit pornographic description. And you're right! The FAP is an epic literary work! Ahhh… Lots of monetary ejaculations in it. Ahhh… (Jane's wacking-off her little clit). Ahhhh… I love reading the **Rise & Fall**. Ahhh…

Jane! Here let me handle you Sweetheart (Mary takes-over jerking Jane's tiny appendage). Hey it's a serious read of American history. Mwah…

Ahhh…. (Jane shoots off a load into Mary's mouth). Ooooh thanks **Mare**. Yeah, yeah, I read some of it, the RFAP is a masterpiece. It depicts the events leading up to why the American male penis got smaller!

Yeah **Jane**. It was at this point where the financially disillusioned American male began to seek alternative sex partners because of the feeling of abandonment by their Mother, aka the US Government. And also due in part to the extreme penalty of castration of his penis if caught and convicted of raping a female in the United States. And rape was defined in the new US Cunt-Stitution as sex with any female which the male was not married to. In other words,

If a man doesn't own it, he can't poke it!

Sure **Mary** where'd you learn this? Bouncing up and down on your Dads Cocklet? (Mary's dad, Samantha is a Sissy-in-Training, SIT).

Yes, Lover in fact I did! On my Daddy's little Sissyology degree educated cum nozzle! My Daddy always talks to me about Sissydom® history when he's making love to me. He told me there was a renaissance of Sissydom because of the disparate post 2008 financial crisis. The desires of American males to poke little boys in the ass increased.

So without the modern day **Vaganus**® to stabilize the situation, the pussy deprived financially destitute American male of course started abusing young male children instead of females. And naturally having been abused financially like debt-slaves since birth they intern abused children because they're the most vulnerable members of society. Mind you this was all in the pre-Homo-Sis-Sapien era.

Geeeezy Weeeezy Mare!

In other words, in the mind's eye of the horny and impoverished American male, their dominance over and subjugation of the weaker and more fragile male child is justified because of the lessons learned from their metaphorically speaking mother-figure, the US Government.

Wow! It was out of control!

Yes, the US government who had be cum an oligarchical monster. Who then financially screwed all of its citizens as if they had been bequeathed the moral rights to screw the American people out of certain unalienable rights of, life, liberty and the pursuit of happiness, otherwise known as property!

So, psychologically, the American male, not including the off the record Gays and government owned Sissies, out of love of their figurative mother, had be cum collectively a gang of pedophiles. The mother, our government, was actually the Cunt-tree they loved and pledged their allegiance too. And the American male pedophile was born out of jealousy of their mother's pimp, which was the privately owned central bank. American men wanted only to prove to their money-whore mother-government, that they too could screw children aka, citizens in the ass as did their pimp father figure the private central bank called the Federal Reserve, the **FED** [23.29].

Huh! It's hard to imagine!

Yeah! And it's through this association of their matriarchal government money-whore with its Pimp-Banker that the, demoralized child also known as, the US male population started down the pedophilia road. In other words, the population wanted to be as perverted as the government that nurtured its perversion.

Wow! Unfucking-believable... (Jane's shaking her head in disbelief).

Ah huh! Historically these were the same Pimp-Bankers who owned the United States Government. The Cunt-gress was owned by the Corporatocracy. They controlled the money-whoring American Government who allured the entire working class of our Cunt-tree into the fractional reserve banker's debt-generating whorehouse of an economy. And by doing so created abject poverty for the bottom 99 percent of the US population after the, 07-08 Financial **Crisis** [23.5.1].

This dysfunctional behavior ultimately caused the American male population to break away from all of the traditional moral convictions and equally as embarrassing, complete abandonment of its belief in the first Constitution of the United States.

Thank you Professor Mary. Okay so let me get this psychology crap straight. Knowing the American males affinity for pedophilia, due in the most part to the not yet existing Sissy Vaganus®, the genetic-engineers in the US National laboratories knew what would be a sexual turn-on for men.

Correct Jane! So the Engineers not only created the **B-Type**® it also designed a Penis Traumatic Shrinkage Drug, the **PTSD** [23.59]. This drug promotes erectile dysfunction causing the male to feel inadequate, diminishes self-worth and reduces human violence.

And of course, they designed the **B-Type** to be a young slutty Gurly-Trap looking **Bitch**® to accommodate the pedophile feelings of the **PTSD**® induced American male. The gene modification drug promotes the growth of a little-boy looking replacements.

Yes **Jane**, although Sissydom® and the MSES are sometimes linked to a Soft-Power Weapon (EN12), a **SPW** [25.31]. But I think it's a bunch of hokum. The Chinese would never do sneaky perverted stuff to fool horny, gullible, Americans! But regardless, hot little young looking Sissy Gurls like you should never be considered Sex-Toys!

HEY! I don't see the problem here! I know I'm a Sex-Toy!

WHAT? Jane!

No! **Mare**, I'm glad I morphed into a pure breed Bitch type Sissy and I like how my body makes me look like I'm a seven year old boy. If my petite little body attracts big strong insecure, hung like a horse, perverted men to me, I'm fine with that! I mean a dick's a dick. I don't care if American's sit around all day jerking-off and fantasize about screwing little children in the ass and makes a decent living wage!

JANE! Wow! How far down the rabbit hole we've cum?

Mary, I think you intellectual types have it all wrong! Just because humanoid Bitch type Sissy® creatures like me have been blessed with bodies the size of a seven year old doesn't mean it's bad to do a Sissy in the ass-puss!

Jane, it only works because Human-Sissy Sex, **HSS**® [7.G1.19] interaction is legal thanks to the adaption of the **Bonobo-Way** [22.19] in the USA Inc. Only under-age Human-to-Human, **HH** [7.G1.15] is dirty sex.

Hell you make it sound like child pornography! When actually, Miss Smarty Pants, Sissy-Sex has been declared a National Sissy Sport, an **NSS**, in the United States for decades. Look it up [4.D-G2.10].

Anyway who cares? At fifty pounds, what's that around 23 kilograms, Stud® men love bouncing me up and down on their super hard fuckpoles! And passing me around, tossing me between them, taking turns doing me. I'm just a little sex-toy for them to play with. And guess what? I LIKE IT!

Wait! Weren't we talking about tits? **Mary**, monster tits like yours in a contact sport like Sissy-Sex® would just get in the way!

Aaaah... **Jane**, the water feels so good on my sore cunt. Hmm... And your tiny little kiddy hand up my twat oooh Baby! Fist me more Jane! (Jane has her arm up Mary's twat up to her elbow). Aaaagh, shove it in Baby! All the way up to your elbow Baby! Aaaaagh! I'm Cumming! Ahhhh...

[1.5] SHOWERS

The Gurls have Stud-Boy company...

Aaagh! Ooooh! Hello there hand! Hey, what's your name?

I'm **Mick** and this is **James** (EN18).

Hey guys, this is **Mary** and I'm **Jane**.

Hey so what's up?

Okay never mind, I see what's up, more ragging hardons. Let me help you keep what's up, up.

Please do by all means. I don't recognize you Sissies.

Slurp, Gak, Gek… (Jane and Mary both immediately got on their knees to perform their duties enthusiastically slurping and sucking away). Guk, Guk... Nice tool Dude!

Are you Gurls new here at FUCIT?

Yeah! Slurp… (Jane responds by taking it out of her mouth briefly). We're really excited, we just moved into our dorm! Guk… Guk… (Jane goes back at it).

Ooooh! Yeah! Like that! Oooh! Yeah… Ahhh…

Gak… Guk… Actually we're freshmen, (Lots of slurping and licking). Mwah… Nice boner! I love big strong Boys! Gek… Glrck…

Ooooh! Of course, because we're seniors. Ahhh…. Yeah…

Gak… Guk… What? (Jane says in a questioning voice).

Me and **James**, we're seniors here at FUCIT. (Mick says).

Guk… Guk… Oh! (Jane still fuzzy about the answer but keeps stroking and sucking the long hard prick). Wait a minute! Aaah! How would you know that exactly?

Jane Honey, don't you get it? They put the new fresh Sissies in the Senior dorms and the old experienced Sissy cunts in with Freshmen boys!

Oh! I get it! Guk, Guk… (More slurping). So, we're fresh meat? Okay this would explain the whole football team screwing our brains out last night! Dah!

And you Sissy's are choice pieces-of-ass, for sure! I'm glad you're in our dorm hall. Aaaagh! Oooh! I gotta put it in **Mary**. You got me so hot Gurl, assume the position?

Sure dude anytime. Just ram it in me big boy! I like it really hard and deep. Aaaagh! Yeah! Do me! Ooooh! (Mary takes his entire shaft). Yeah! Yeah!

Mary, I love your enormous tits! You look like a real classy Sissy Lady! Mary! Who owns you? Does a Stud have dibs on you? Mwah… Mwah…

No **James**! Nobody has a claim on me, I'm a free Gurl. Mwah… Ahhhh… Harder! Fuck-me!

You're tits are so big! Aaaagh! I love you, you fine looking Sissy DOM! Kisss… Kisss… Yeah! Mwah…

Ooooh! It's your dick talking James! Shut-up! And do me! Mwah… Mwah… Ahhh…Yeah! Yeah! Yeah!

Oh! You handsome animal! Aaaaagh! I feel so good! Ahhh…

Take me Mary! Take it! Aaaagh! Oooh that was soooo.... good! Mary I jizzed your hole! I'm sooo horny for you! Kisss...

Thank you! Ahhh... It was wonderful James! Oooh! Big load! Ummm... (Mary reaches between her legs and scoops up a Jizz-wad, then swallows it down). Ummm... Tasty! Mwah...

Mick & Jane...

Wow! **Jane**, you don't waste any time, (Jane jumps up into the young man's arms, wraps her legs around his waist and settles down onto his throbbing erection).

Oooh! Aaaagh! **James** she's a wild little Sissy!

Yeah! She just jumped up onto me and started hiding!

She's a little cock-loving monkey!

Yeah! Thump... thump... thump... this one's wild! Thump... thump... This is going to be a great year! Best ever! Aaagh! Ride me Bitch! Thump... thump (Jane rides him to orgasm with her feet planted firmly on his large muscular thighs).

Pop a load Dude! Ahhhh.... Ahhh... Mwah... Ummm...

Whoohooo! Ride it Cow-Gurl! Aaagh! Yeah! There she blows! Aaaagh! Yeah! Nice screw Jane! You petite little fuck-monkey!

Oh bitch you're the best! Mwah... Mwah... Mwah...

Mick, nice dick dude! (Jane slurps up cum wads from his softened appendage). Tasty too! Hmm. Mary Hmmm...

Babe snowball me **Jane**, (Both Gurls reach between their legs push out of their ass-pussies the fresh creamy loads plus their Sissy poop). Kiss... Ummm... Tasty treat! Ummm....

Here **Mare**, eat this wad of love-cream I collected for you. Show me you love me, swallow it Lover!

Glrck... Ummm... Yummy, Yummy! Yeah, now take my load and poop out of my Sissy-Puss **Jane**, swallow it my precious little Bitch! Swallow it Baby! (Jane takes it all down her throat).

Glrck... Guk... Ummm... You taste sooo good Mare! Mwah... Mwah... Love you!

Uoooo, Good Gurl! Mwah... Mwah... I love you too Jane.

Mary, kiss me! Eat my load Mary! Mwah...

I love you too **Jane** my horny little Bitch®. Kiss.... Kissss... Look Babe. (Mary opens her mouth to prove to Jane she swallowed the whole load). Ummmm So good! I love eating your Poop! Mwah...

[1.6] POOP

The Boys freak-out about eating Sissy-Poop...

Uoooh! How can you guys stomach eating cum wades mixed with the shit out of your ass? Aghhh! That's gross!

Yeah James has a point Gurls. The Sperm I can see that! But your enthusiasms for swallowing poop not so much.

Oh Dudes, it only proves how great this Cunt-trie is! The scientist here in the United States Inc. thought of everything when they designed us Homo-Sis-Sapiens. You see, our shit otherwise known as **Sissy-Poop**® [4.D-G1.37] tastes like male sperm. And it's extremely nutritious and tastes great.

You sure about that? (The Boys look on with perplexed looks on their faces).

Ah huh! We're American Sissies, even our frats smell good! I mean our shit is actually a patented product. The **Poop**® is the best tasting in the world thanks to American Bio-Engineering. Heck! Jane and I always eat each other's Poop out of our **Vaganus**® [14.O1.6] holes, we rarely use a toilet.

Ooouuugh, Gross! Ugh... Unbelievable! It's amazing but disgustingly scary at the same time. I mean the thought of eating shit is not on my list of things to do in my life.

Well yeah because you Boys are human. Jane and I are Hono-Sis-Sapien, we're not humans. We only look like humans. In actuality we're classified by the US Department of Agriculture as an alien livestock animal. Oh! And its **Sissy-Poop**® [4.D-G1.37] not shit. The USA Inc. owns the patent on what cums out of our Vaganus®. Besides, the correct categorization is, humans shit, Sissies poop.

Well, yeah shit, poop whatever, I guess animals in nature don't use toilets. But Pssss... You guys are hot looking chick.

Yeah! Mick is right! Hey I'll just close my eyes when you Gurls eat each other out!

Right, the only time I do use a toilet to take-a-poop is when Jane's been a bad Sissy Gurl and screws around without my permission. When this happens I just refuse her the privilege of eating my poop load.

Wow! Okay, I'm getting weak in the stomach listening to this. You disciple Jane by refusing her your Poop? You gotta admit, it sounds a bit sadistic! Haa ha…

Ahhhhh… Maybe. But Jane is funny, she'll pout for days when I do that, but she's a good little Bitch® I think I'm gonna keep her. I mean, I've never had to put a leach on her or beat her. The only thing she likes more than my Sissy-Poop® is long hard penis. Mwah… Mwah…

[1.7] DOM-BITCH

Talk about the Dom-Bitch marital issues….

Well anyway, hey, let's party again sometime? Mwah…

Definitely Dude! You guys are a blast! Mwah…

Hey we're Whorehouse® WH069S in suite 069, so please pop-in and pop-off a load anytime guys. You're more than well cum to mount us! Mwah… Kisss…

Sure **Jane** and it was good meeting you too Mary. (Mick says).

Yeah, hey guys, maybe next time you guys can share us both. (Although not really what Mary is into, she suggests a group activity).

For sure **Mary**, sharing is, a great suggestion, I always share. So, talk about sharing, you guys seem pretty tight together (Jane and Mary are standing there with their arms locked around each other). Are you guys married?

Oh, no! Well, we could get married now with the new dual-marriage law called the DOM-Bitch Marriage, **DBM**® [6.C]. The new law lets Sissies get married to each other as long as they eventually get Sissy-Breeder married and breed Sissies with a Sissy breeding human female wife.

Wow! Okay, so you still would need to breed Sissies?

Well yeah! Bitches or DOMs but the **SBP** [4.D-G6.2] assigns a breeding bitch to you based on family cock-lineage. Us Sissies don't even have to go looking for a breeding wife.

Oh okay that makes sense. I just assumed you two had tied the knot because you're so close. You guys hold hands kiss and hug each other and you even snowball cum loads. And oddly enough your shit, Uooogh! I can't get the image out of my mind. Agh!

Hmmm... Mwah... Yeah we do love each other. Oh and its call Poop, humans shit, Sissies Poop. And we're bonded?

What do mean bonded? (James asks).

We've taken our **Sissy-Promise**® [6.F.A.1] vows together. So, I guess it makes us a couple, but we're not married yet. Just Bonded! And I love her sooo much Mwah...

Oh, ok, so the Sissy-Promise® is like being engaged to be married?

Yeah, yeah... Something like that. The Bitch® vows she can't screw-around with other Sissies without the DOMs permission. And I guess if a DOM only has one Bitch you can consider it a pretty serious relationship. Jane's my only Bitch. And you can tell she's promised by the bow around her clit. It's supposed to be a warning to other Sissies that she's spoken for.

Well anyway, I'm looking forward to having more special times with you guys. And hey, we're in the universities marching band so we have hundreds of friends we can share with you. Hint! Hint!

Oooh! Direct approach, I like that! Well, **Mick**, I don't know.

Oh, why don't you know Mary?

You see, hundreds of hormonal ragging male Studs, for me and Jane, we usually don't bother with such a small group.

Hooo! Ok wow! Well we'll just bring the marching band and the football team with us. Ha... ha... haaa...

Cool! Yeah well Jane's up for it of course, but Mick I was just kidding with you. Being a DOM I'm not as promiscuous as Jane.

Ahhhh... Hmmm... Mary so why does Jane get excited about the massive gangbang offer and you're not?

Mick, you realize I'm a DOM® and Jane's a Bitch®, right?

Ahhhh... You kinda lost me there, Mary. I'm not too sure that that means actually.

Well, you know we both love being the center of attention but a big gangbang is more Jane's style because she's a B-Type. But I'm a DOM Sissy and I like to have more of a one-on-one thing with Studs! Now don't get me wrong, even though DOM type Sissies always have a smaller **Cockage**® number than the Bitch type, I still like to pull-a-train. I mean I'll do a small gang but only one man at a time. I just like intimate romantic sex more than the gangbang brute force type where all the guys just pile on top of the Gurl.

Alright! Sounds good to me, Mary and you're definitely a fine Sissy Lady for sure. Maybe we can go out on a date sometime?

Sure Mick, I date Studs but hey, just me and you, don't invite all your friends.

Sure, sure… Mary, just you and me. But Mary what about Jane? I mean, you guys are obviously hooked-up?

Oh Jane? Huh! She's my Bitch. So she knows her place. If we go out on a date together, Jane will behave herself and wait by the door for me to cum home like a good Bitch is supposed to.

Okay, I guess I'm starting to understand the DOM-Bitch thing you were talking about. So what are you doing Saturday night Mary?

I guess going on a romantic date with a big handsome college Stud dude. Kiss…

Kiss… I'll pick you up around eight?

Sure Mick (Mary squeezes Mick's dick). It'll be fun!

Well you two are awesome! Mwah… We'll see you guys around. (The boys say good bye to Mary and Jane with satisfied smiles on their faces and empty nut-sacks). Mwah… Mwah…

Mwah… Okay, see yah!

[1.9] FIRST-DAY

Freshmen year, first class…

First day of class, first year of college, we made it Mary!

I know Lover. Jane can you please stop eating my sex trainers load out of my hole. We have to get to class, Honey-Bunny!

No! Ummm…. It's sooo delicious (Jane ignores the warning and keeps slurping away at Mary). Gulp… **Mare** I love eating out your sweet Sissy cunt! Hmm... Gulp... Mwah...

Stop it **Jane**! We gotta go!

Sure okay, but your **Vaganus**® goo mixed with Sissy-Poop® tastes so good! Show me how much you love me, poop in my mouth Baby! Shit in your Bitches mouth, I love you! Mwah… Ahhh…

SLAP! Jane? Let's not make this a lesson in proper Bitch conduct. We're gonna be late!

Yeah Baby slap me again, I surrender to you. I love you! Slap your Bitch! Ugh! (Jane gets off on the discipline Mary provides her).

No! No more! Jane Honey, come-on let's just douche-out and go we can't be late for Sissyology class. Jane if you're good today I'll poop in your mouth later when we get back from class.

Okay Mare! Ummm… Yummy treats later. (Jane, even though she has an IQ higher than 200 still loves to feel like a child when dominated by Mary).

Ahh isn't it great we can have a dorm suite big enough for us and our sex trainers?

Oh yeah it's quite accommodating of the **FUCIT** [3.C1.4] to provide this much space and full Sissyed out rooms with deluxe **Douche-a-Matic**® 2500 [4.D-G1.23] models, one for each of us.

Also these two king size beds, provides plenty of room for us and our training studs.

Yeah and the best part was being able to hold each other in our arms while our **SST** Sissy Sex Trainers [4.D-G3.1] service us.

Yeah, side-ways as we were waking up. Ooooh yeah Jane! Kissss... Mwah… The FUCIT is an awesome school.

Ah huh! This is a great school. Mwah… And hey! I love sleeping in your arms Mary. Hmmm... Oh Wildflower, I adore you. We're going to be in each other's arms forever. Kiss..... Kisssss… You're so precious to me **Mare**. Mwah…

Mwah… Oh Sweetheart! We'll be together through the years. I just feel, as Sissies we've been given such a wonderful opportunity. I mean, just look at all this Whorehouse® equipment with a Labor Compensation Benches, **LCB**® [22.4] for both of us and they're adjustable so we can side them next to each other.

Yeah, making it easy for us Sissy students to study together while performing our Whorehouse obligations. And the special Vaganus® only rule is great!

Oh yeah! Jane it's only for Student Whorehouses, **S-Type** [7.G4.S] so we can refuse blow-job service to Studs if we're studying during the Whorehouse hours.

Right! Cause it's hard to read a textbook with a dick in your mouth.

Oh! And don't forget the maid-service for Sissy dorm rooms. Sure! I love the cleaning service when the maid eats-out my screwed twat.

And the extra big walk-in closets for all of our, FuckMe® cloths and **SissyGear**®. Talk about cloths? Is that all you're wearing Jane? You're practically naked!

Geeezzz… Mary you sound like my Mother.

But really Jane, a cup-less bra, lace-top stays-up stockings, a skirtini and six-inch pumps.

You forgot my pretty frilly lacy Cum-Sock® (Jane making a childish smile while posing as a model).

Ha! Ha! (Mary push's Jane out the door). Let's just go my little petite scantily clad Bitch® before we're late for class!

Yes, Miss Domination. Mwah… Your wish is my cum-mand!

[1.10] STROLLING

Swaying through campus on the way to class…

Mary! Check-out the hot Sissy Bitch, hey Gurl! (Jane shouts across the yard at a hot looking Bitch type).

Hey what's up? (The Sissy seductively blows an air-kiss back at Jane). Mwah…

God-of-Cocks, **Jane**, I swear I'm gonna have to tighten your leash if you start hitting on the other Bitches here at college.

Yes Boss! Ha… haa... And you should talk, you made a date with a **Stud**® dude and you didn't even ask me if it was alright. But NO! I can't play with the other horny Bitches. Talk about double standards.

Jane, DOMs don't have to ask for permission from their Bitches for anything.

Mary, you don't see me hitting on DOMs do you? I just go for other Bitches. I'm faithful to Mary. Mwah… I'm not looking for a DOM, I got one! But hey! Some playtime sex with a hot Bitch, yeah! Look at all these hot college Bitches!

I know **Jane**, these B-Type Gurls are hot, but this is college, so can you please just tone down the whorishness?

Yes, cum-man-her Mary!

Wow I'm beginning to like college already.

Whys that Mary?

Because Jane, there're rules here.

Geeez… Did you have to say the **R** word? I hate when you swear like that. Ha haaa... Rules! Agh!

What's wrong with rules Jane? Other than you don't believe they should exist.

Mare, I like rules, just not the one's pertaining to sex!

Haa haaa ha… Very funny my Lover, very funny. Mwah…

Okay Mary, what rules do you like at our college?

The ones which keep the boys from mounting us anywhere and anytime they want. We have to focus on our studies. We're not kids anymore (Mary has always been more serious than Jane).

This is the worst rule! Restricting sex, there should be a law against rules like that! (Jane says while Mary drags her by the hand to class).

Yeah, but without those kinds of Sex-Rules we would never get to class on time, just look at all these Studs® walking around. Hell we would never get to class!

Okay, you got a point Mary. Check-out those hardons!

Yes **Jane**, my point exactly! Ignore their erections! College is challenging, especially when you have a Gurlfriend who won't stop eating out your cunt when you're trying to leave on time for class!

Heee.... heeee... I can't help it, you taste sooo good! Mwah...

Mwah... Well **Jane**, I guess college is a good change for us. It's different, more mature, like less fooling around in the halls and in the boy's restrooms between classes. The sex is still there if we want it.

Yeah, yeah... All we have to do is walk into any of the Whoring Stations here on campus and bend over for as many penetrations as we want. Easy Peasy!

Yep! Gurlfriend, this is the good life. Mwah...

And hey, you're looking super-hot Mary. These guys are looking at you and drooling. Huh!

Thank you Babe. Hmmm... Kiss... Yeah, they stare at me a lot.

You're always dress to impress Gurl. The Lady power-suite and the short-skirt with the exposed clit slit in the front. Your big boobs in a lacy shelf bra, the see through top, the grater-belt, lace-top stockings and with six-inch classic pumps, jewelry, it's just such a real Classic Whore look.

Thank you Baby. Kisss... You say the sweetest things to me. Mwah...

You're beautiful! And sophisticated Mary. Kisss... You always have a sexy, *do me if you can,* look. I love being with you and holding your hand. Noticing the other Sissy Bitches looking at me with a real jealous look after checking you out.

Oh Jane! Mwah... You're mine, I don't need another.

You're sooo hot Babe, you're a hot classy Sissy Whore Lady and I'm lucky to be your Bitch. I love you Mary, Umm... kissss... kiss... (Jane says in a deprecating tone as she clings to Mary).

I love you too my trampy little child-looking Bitch. Mwah... You always have a young and sexy seductive Whore® look about you. You're such a piece of jail-bait **Jane**. Mwah...

[1.11] MARRIAGE

Oh **Jane** I love when you brag about me like that, let's get Sissy-Married? I love you sooo much! Mwah...

Oooh Babe! Yes, Yes, Yes, I will marry you! I've always loved you **Mare**, I've been bonded to you since before pre-school.

Oh **Jane**, hug-me, kiss-me, never let go! Mwah...

Mwah... I won't let go Mary. (Jane wraps her arms around Mary). I'll love my DOM forever! Mwah...

Mwah… And after all these years of loving each other we can legally get married, isn't it so wonderful to be a Sissy?

Oh definitely! Mwah… And the married Sissies can even share their breeding wives with each other too.

Okay, I'll knock-up yours if you knock-up mine! Isn't it cool?

Baby only in America! We're in the right place at the right time. Married Sissies can screw each other's breeding wife. And nowhere else on the planet is this possible! Cross-Genome breeding, this is like living in a sci-fi movie.

Yes my Darling! It's a fantasy come true! Sissies older then eighteen can now legally be in a Sissy-Marriage. And I knew after we made our Sissy-Promise® to each other we would be soul-mates forever. We'll soon make plans and tell our parents when the time is right, maybe on winter break.

Okay Lover (Jane & Mary stroll to their class holding hands tightly, shoulder to shoulder).

Yea! Let's get to class we'll have all the time in the world to plan a wonderful **Cockolic** [9] Sissy wedding.

[1.12] SISSYOLOGY

First class…

Well cum to Sissyology 101. My name is Professor **Yaoi**. (The Professor is a sensuous looking, voluptuous, full-figured women dressed very conservatively). Many of you are in this class because you're Sissies training to be cum Professional Sissy Whores in the **MSES®** [4.D-G2.1]. And it requires you to major in Sissyology for your managerial careers in the Whoring

Industry. Some of you are majoring in it to have one of the many careers in the nationwide Sissy support industry. All of these careers are growing exponentially and faster than any other. So if you're not majoring in Sissyology, I'm afraid you're missing the boat my young friends.

Okay so let's get started. This question might seem like a redundant one and I'm sure you've all answered it many times in the past. But I want college level answers here. And leave out the parts about how Sissies are mutated out of test tubes in a laboratory from monkey DNA, it's irrelevant. This is a two-part question, (1) why do we have Sissies in our society? I mean, why do we breed them into existences and (2) why are Sissy people so important to us today in our MSES? And just a reminder, the MSES here in the United States of America Incorporated and Sissydom®, is one in the same.

Yes the scantily clad tiny little Sissy here in the front (The Professor points at Jane while scanning her childlike body).

My name is **Jane** Professor, Jane Goldberg.

Okay Jane, go ahead answer the questions young lady.

Well, Sissies are part of the Modern Socio-Economic System. The **MSES** [4.D-G2.1]. We were created in the post Federal Reserve (FED) era, in the new United States. (2) It's proven to be the ultimate solution to the previously failed, non-constitutional, fraudulent, privately owned, fiat money spewing, and factional reserve banking system called the Financial Enslavement Dicks, or the **FED** [4.D-G4.17].

Wow! You said all that in one breathe. Very impressive for a fragile little, prepubescent scrawny looking stick persons like you. (Professor Yaoi says as she frowns down on Jane).

Thank you Professor. And I wasn't finished with part one. (Jane fearfully remarks).

Wow! There's more! Go on than!

Yes Professor Yaoi! (Jane says as she timidly looks up at the statuesque Professor towering over her). The FED was supported by the 16th amendment which imposes in cum tax on earned labor which is actually the definition of slavery. The FED members were all criminals known for their atrocities against humanity. Millions of innocent people perished because of the debt-peonage resulting from the dollar hegemony of the FED!

Okay, okay, let me interject here class (Yaoi interrupts Jane). In sight of there being no currency to barter with in the post FED era, Sissies were brought into existence. Go on. Huh! And please stop playing with your snatch while you're speaking young lady.

Sorry Professor. Yes, Sissies were created to maintain a strong workforce by providing sex as a bartering mechanism. The breed and non-breed Sissy culture supplies workers with sexual pleasures as well as Labor Compensation Transactions or **LCT** [4.D-G2.27] for short. The LCT is monetary compensation for a workers labor. And the replacement of the sex industries female prostitutes with Sissies has liberated the Sissy and Stud breeding human women. This enabled them to give birth to more workers and whores, which increased the GDP of the USA Inc.

Part (2) of your question Professor, Sissies also provide a benefit to society, culturally speaking, by integrating hetero, homo and bisexual oriented people together to create a unified, productive, financially controlled yet very sexually active society. This was accomplished with the creation of the twenty-ninth amendment, which defines the new morality rules set forth in the Second, yet to be ratified, United States Incorporated Cunt-Stitution [17].

May I continue Professor?

Again wow! Lots of factual information, yes please do continue. By all means. Huh! I'm gonna step out for a coffee, this might take a while…

Haa haaa haa (The whole class erupts in a laugh).

Thank you Professor. For example after Sissydom was created by the **Sissification Act** [1.0] and the American people embraced the new morality or lack thereof. Crime has almost been eliminated. The **USA Inc.** [0.0] now has the lowest crime rate of any Cunt-tree in the world with the exception of China. And (Jane turns to all her classmates, in the large lecture hall, of a hundred or more students and throws her chest out proudly, tweaking her exposed budding nipples for all of them to see and shouts out), as a Sissy I'm proud to be a WHORE!

Yay! Sissy Pride! Whoohooo! Applause.... Applause... Clap, clap… (All her classmates clap in agreement).

In the greatest Nation on Earth! This is the new America! I'm so full of pride (Jane removes her clit sock and throws her arms in the air as her sock-less clit spews Jizzies high into the air). I know as a Sissy I'm a productive member of society!

Clap, clap… Clap, clap… Right on! Yay! (More applauses and shouting slogans). Whoohooo! We have rights! Yay! Clap, clap… clap…

I'm glad to have been genetically modified and then re-classified from common feminine male to a sensuous female Sissy Gurl and give my body up for my Cunt-tree! Whoohooo!

SISSY'S RULE! (Shouts an anonymous voice from high up in the lecture hall). Yeah! Yeah! Yah! Whoohooo! Power-to-Sissies! We're proud!

Okay, that's enough! Settle down! (Yaoi tries to calm down the class as they enthusiastically applaud), folks. Settle down.

Yay! You're HOT Jane! Wheeee! Whooo! (Studs admiring Jane and whistle at her).

That's enough! Calm down.

Some minutes later….

Thank you young lady! That was well spoken. Calm down everybody and please take your seats. Thank you again Ms. **Goldberg**, well put. And sorry young lady, I'm going to have to write you up for a Sissy and Stud Sperm Management infraction. The **SSSM** [4.D-G2.9] is a Federal rule.

Sorry Professor. (Jane hangs her head and flops back down in the seat next to Mary then under her breath says). Huh! What a domineering jerk!

Shhhh…. (Mary puts her arm around Jane to quiet her down). Jane, let's not make any waves here at FUCIT. Yaoi is one of the top Professors. Mwah… She's a department head.

[1.13] SISSY-SEX

Wow! That was something, quite a response. I don't usually see Sissies with this kind of moxie. Real boldness, very impressive. Okay, now class, answer this question, why does the USA Inc. government use Sissy-Sex or sometimes called **Sissy-Love** [15-69.7] as part of its worker compensation system?

Hmm... Maybe... Ahhh... Uhhh... Well ahh... Huh? (The auditorium of students is grumbling loudly, trying to piece together a response).

Okay, let me reword that! I mean, why doesn't the government just print fiat make-believe, funny-money, currency like they did after the 2008 Financial **Crisis** [23.5.1]. This was before the collapse of the US dollar and its hegemony as the world's reserve currency. Why doesn't the Government just drop money from helicopters onto the workers?

Yes, up in the back, the Stud looking fellow with the massive pec muscles. (The buff looking Stud student stands up). Yes you!

Professor, it's because our government and every other empire has done the same thing in the past and it fails every time. The fiat currencies only have a value proportionally related to the amount of fear which can be instilled into the holders of the IOU notes of currency. For example, if the Cunt-tree printing the fiat currency has a large military and domestic security force, then it can set a value of the currency based on its ability to brainwash the fear of death into the holders of the currency.

Okay, this was a very good answer and without any titillation of any kind. (The Professor looks at Jane sternly).

Haa haaa haa... Heee (Again the whole class erupts in a laugh about Jane's lewd performance) Haa haaa... Janie!

Class this is true, because fear has been used as a financial weapon or what we call a Soft-Power Weapon, a **SPW** [25.31]. These have been used by every imperialistic empire on earth. For example, the old United States was a master at bullying other nations with economic sanctions at the barrel of a gun. Or if necessary, send in the militarily for an intervention by replacing the current democratically elected ruler with a new US puppet government as in the Cunt-tree of **Ukame** [25.36a], the previous Ukraine. Sadly in the case of Ukame, the US President at the time was this douche-bag called Donald Trump. The House of Representatives was smart enough to catch him trying to pull a Quid-Pro-Quo scam on them. He was **Imp-Eached** [23.8.2] and then later exiled to Baltimore.

Hmmm... (Professor Yaoi relaxes while pondering the next question. She strolls over to where the Gurls are seated. Then, while licking her lips and for no apparent reason gives Jane a wink of approval).

Mare! Did you see that? She winked at me! What do you think that means? (Jane says under her breath).

Shhhh.... Quiet down Jane. It's weird, but it looked like a wink you get from a guy who's tries to pick you up in a bar.

Okay! Now, here's another two part question. If this is the reasoning behind being able to print fiat currency, why does the fear tactic always fail? And why not just do it the old way and provide Non-Sissy human females for the workers to have sex with instead of genetically modified experimental freaks like Sissies?

Yes, the elegant Sissy Lady here in the front with the large bosom next to Jane our liberated and boastingly proud Sissy Gurl.

Professor (Mary stands up to respond). Currency eventually losses its make-believe, propagandized value and people stop trusting in it's worth. This happens when the faith is broken between the State and its people, it fails. In other words it be cums worthless because its value was based on faith like a religious belief.

And faith in a Ponzi scheme type of monetary system based on fiat currency is always broken due to the deceitful nature of a scheme itself. The old US Oligarchical government, which in reality was not a Cunt-tree or government at all, but an enterprise owned and operated by the **FED**. This pseudo supposedly American government had supported this Ponzi scheme prior to the Second **Cunt-Stitution** [17] to maintain financial control over the populace aka impoverished working class. (Mary pauses).

Go on young Lady. (Yaoi gives her approval to continue).

Ponzi schemes swindle hard working people out of their savings. Only the rich benefit from fractional reserve banking schemes because they're on the top of the pyramid. The rest of the ninety-nine percent of the population suffers because they're in financial debt to the one percent forever. And the private sector debt is almost never cancelled. There is supposed to be some kind of a **Debt-Jubilee** [21.B.15]. But in modern times this rarely happens. Only the Banks are relieved of their debt.

Mary! Can you just focus on the fait currency please? Thank you.

Certainly Professor. So regardless of how large a government's army or its quantitative easing to the Banks is, people just don't like having little or no opportunity. And contrary to the bourgeoisie opinion, people aren't stupid, regardless of how poor they are or how many guns are pointed at them, people listen to their hearts. If they can't afford to raise and feed a family then they know something's wrong.

Okay! And about the human Whores? (Yaoi blurts out).

Right! The second part of your question Professor Yaoi, why not provide workers sex with human females? Well, yeah, females naturally provide sex comparably if not better than most Sissies can. Although there are ongoing studies by **Hardon-Vard** University [21.C.12] and others like the one being conducted here at FUCIT which are testing if the American male prefers Sissy **Vaganus**® [14.O1.6] otherwise known as ass-pussy to that of human female vagina aka pussy.

Yes! I was a co-author of this study (Yaoi brags).

And just the fact that women have three holes and Sissies having been genetically redesigned from Bonobo monkeys and male Homo-Sapiens DNA into **Hono-Sis-Sapien** [18.3], only have two holes for penetration gives human females a bias 2 to 3 sexual advantage.

But also there's a pregnancy issue here in the Modern Socio-Economic System of the United States Inc. As my friend Jane so proudly (Jane is between Mary's legs with her fist up her Vaganus) mentioned. Aaaagh! The fe... fee... feem... females Aaagh... In the MSES are needed to breed worker and whore babies which is something the vagina-less, gene mutated, Sissies cannot perform.

Young Lady, please pause to have your orgasm. FUCIT is an Integrated Sex School [11]. This makes it perfectly acceptable for a student to pause momentary for a proper orgasm.

Thank you Professor! Aghh... Yeah! (Jane pulls her dainty little arm out of her lover and Mary presses her legs together while shivers in the throes of her intense orgasm). Ummm...

You may continue when ready (Yaoi says with a smirk and yawns about the relieved look on Mary's face).

Huh… (Mary is still kinda out of breath). This of course makes Sissies virtually useless for anything but sex. I mean sure, us Sissies have a high IQ are great fun at parties and in bed. And men like taking turns screwing us and everything, but in reality, our one virtue in life is to give the male workers monetary compensation for their hard work. And it was appropriate and genius of the new United States Inc. Government to utilize the patented **Vaganus**®.

Clap… Clap… Clap… (The class breaks out proudly in an approving round of applause). Yay! Clap… Clap…

In our full capacity as sex providers!

Clap… Clap… (More applause).

Sex as a reward! For all of our hard working men here in the new America!

Clap… Clap… Yay! Yeah! (Mary waves her hands to the rest of the class acknowledging their praise while erupting into several orgasms). Clap… Clap…

Several minutes later…

Truly spoken. Thank you Miss? My name is Mary Dune.

Thank you Ms. Dune. Very nice response to the questions.

Thank you Ms. Yaoi, I mean Professor.

So, on to the next question, how is replacing fear with sex going to provided help to anything? And no stupid sexist remarks on this question please! This is a university not a preschool.

Haaaa.... haaa... ha... ha... (Student laughter).

Yes, the Barbie looking Non-Sissy gal way in the back, speak loudly so we can all hear you please.

Sex is succeeding as a measure of wealth because, in the mind of your typical highly intelligent human, sex is more valuable than gold or silver. So when a man ejaculates his sperm into a Sissy which is really just another form of sadism because the pussy of a Sissy is really just a male asshole constructed from DNA, which by-the-way has been widened to make it feel like the guy is having intercourse with a real female vagina, this makes him feel gratified, not only by performing sodomy on the vulnerable dumb-ass Sissy but also reaffirming his masculinity by taking advantage of the submissive Sissy boys ass, this demonstrates his mastery of being a productive wealthy American Stud, he is then of course compensated for his hard work with a deposit into his bank account when he ejaculates his precious Man-Cream into the animals anal cavity, aka, Sissy freaks butt-hole and then the strong, masculine, superior man...

Booo! Bo.... Booo... Cunt! Booo... Bigot! Booo... (The Sissy students are all up on their feet shouting in disapproval).

Yes, yes, that will be all! Thank you young Stud lady! For this long, spiteful, biased, detailed twisted opinion. It was more of a manifesto on how much you hate Sissies than an answer to my question. But thank you none-the-less for your rant. And how you said all of that in one breath I'm not quite sure.

Ha... haa... haa... haa... Yeah! (Student laughter and heckling). Wacko! Huh! Dumb cunt! Ha... haa...

That's enough! Oh by the way, it's called a **Vaganus**® not an anal cavity. And NO it's not a butt-hole or poop-chute. And for your own edification you should try one of the Sissy-Poop® gourmet dishes in the FUCIT cafeteria, Ummm... Kisss... Absolutely delicious!

Ha... haa... haa... (More student laughter).

So yes class, sex is the most wanted thing on earth believe it or not. And it's regardless of the hole being penetrated. Human vagina or American Pure Sissy **Vaganus**®, it really doesn't matter. And it's a shame millions of people have died in wars fought over nothing to do with sex. Think about it, no one would have died in wars if we all had one big orgy to resolve our conflicts!

Ha, hah! Ha... Hah... Haaa... Haa… (The whole class breaks out laughing again).

Yeah! For example, the **Bonobo** [18.0.1] monkeys in Africa, who the Sissy creatures are fashioned after, resolve conflicts with sexual contact. It's us the humans who are the violent freaks of nature. Not the peace loving Hono-Sis-Sapien Sissies we share the MSES with.

Here in the USA Inc. we're doing more for world peace through the use of sex than any other Cunt-tree. Take the American invention of the Vaganus® which made sex so abundant in our Cunt-tree. And to a small extent made it available to our subjugated territories in the north, Canada and south in the Americas. In those impoverished places, which we conquered in back in 2069, it's only a matter of time till they succumb to the powerful influence of the patented American **Vaganus**®. As they had previously to the American dollar.

Well that's it for today class! And don't forget to read your assignment 6.9 on the difference between Sissies and Prostitutes aka Lobbyists.

Oh! You two! (Being stopped by the professor has Jane and Mary feeling like they just got caught cheating on a test). Yes, Mary and Jane, can I have a word with you both?

Us Professor, do you want to speak with us?

Are we in trouble Mary? What did we do wrong?

Shhhh…. Nothing Jane, hold my hand and please try not to pop a load while she's speaking to us. (Mary marches them back to where the Professor is waiting for them).

[1.14] PROPOSAL

Yaoi invites the Gurls to the NSA proposal…

Yes you two cum, **Mary** and **Jane**. (Yaoi motions them to cum back to her by pointing at them and moving her index finger repeatedly). Yes please cum closer. Huh! I don't bite. I just wanted to have a word with the two of you real quick.

Did we do something wrong Professor **Yaoi**? Ma'am I'm sorry about throwing my chest out (Jane sheepishly says with her head down), but I'm just so proud to be a Sissy. I can't help myself.

No…. no… no… My sweet dear Gurl! (Yaoi bends over takes Jane's tiny little head in her hands and gives a peck on her forehead). Mwah… Quite the contrary, I wanted to thank you.

Thank you both. You two were the spark the class needed. Huh! (Yaoi opens her eyes wide, brings her arms up to her protruding large chest, clinches her fists and shakes them as a sign of power). You lead the parade!

Thanks Professor Yaoi.

It was really brave to get up in front of that many **Stud**® students and speak as eloquently as colorful as you two have today. And your responses to my questions were right on target and well spoken. This was also a display of your academic prowess and aptitude. Making me glad you both flew your Sissy flag. It will serve as an act of affirmation of you both being proud of whom you are. You have pride in yourselves as Sissy **Gurls**® and as Americans. It's good to see this.

Thank you Ms. **Yaoi**. Thank you Professor Yaoi (The Gurls with an idolizing stares, mouths wide open, are mesmerized by this tall domineering Amazon beauty). It was nothing Professor. (Mary, head down, says in a deprecating tone).haa ha!

Not so nothing, my Dear! I want you to know it's rare for Sissy-Gurls to be as brave as you were. And because of this I have a proposal (Mary and Jane look at each other confused) for the both of you.

Huh, for us Professor? (Mary asks frowning in disbelief).

Yes! The two of you obviously do not lack self-esteem. I'm this university's Chairperson for the National Sissydom Association, the **NSA** [4.D-G6.13]. And I have two internships and scholarships available for Sissies like yourselves who have shown an extraordinary ability to do public speaking on topics related to **Sissydom**®. I want you to think about my offer and if you're interested, we can schedule a meeting so I can explain what your responsibilities would be.

Sure Professor **Yaoi**, we, I mean I think we (Mary turns to Jane for her approval and Jane enthusiastically shakes her head yes) would be honored to be part of the largest Sissy® orgasmization in the world.

That's great Gurls! Oh! Did I mention it would involve traveling to give speeches and demonstrations at other colleges and to the Cunt-gress in Washingcum DC? So the positions are very demanding and also exciting.

Wow! Professor, we would be grateful to you for the offer.

Oh! Yes, we'll talk about gratuities later. And you'll both be giving Sissy-Sex® demonstrations in front of large stadium audiences. But judging by the way you two handled the auditorium of students today I don't think you'll have much of a problem. Uooh! One more thing, in the demonstrations all of the Stud® men in the audience participate by penetrating you.

Oh God-of-Cocks! (Mary is lactating from the excitement). Professor Yaoi, I don't know what to say!

Good then! Well, cum by my office Friday after your last class, I have a short test which I know you'll both pass easily and application papers for you both to sign.

Thanks again Professor, Thanks. We'll see yah then. Friday in this office Professor! (The Gurls excitedly get up to leave the office).

Okay Gurls. Oh and Gurls! The meeting might take several hours on Friday, so you might want to post on the FUCIT

Whorehouse® (WH) website a schedule change stating you won't be open for business on Friday night.

Okay for sure Prof Yaoi! (The Gurls are all-a-glee with enthusiasm). Can do! We're so happy! See yah Professor Yaoi. (The Gurls exit the office door and begin to skip away joyously).

[1.15] POTION

Yaoi has a private conversation with Jane…

Jane! Jane, Sweetheart! (The Gurls only get a partially down the hall when Yaoi shouts and motions with her hand for Jane to cum back to her. Then Jane, as if she was an obedient puppy dog, gladly runs back to hear what the Professor has to say).

Yes Prof? At your service! (Jane smiles ear to ear and jumps to attention, while kiddingly military salutes the Professor).

Haa ha… Oh! So adorably cute! Yes! You're my little Soldier Gurls. Mwah… (As a salute back Yaoi blows an air-kiss at Jane). Mary, can I talk to Jane in private for a moment, please?

Ahhh… Sure Professor Yaoi (Mary is caught off guard by Yaoi's desire to speak with her Gurlfriend).

Mary, I'll catch up to you. Mwah…

Mwah… Okay Jane! I'll walk slowly. (Then Mary whispers to Jane). But I kinda wonder what Yaoi has to say to you that she can't say to both of us?

Jane my Dear! In my office please.

Yes Prof Yaoi? Cuming!

Yaoi closes the office door behind them...

Jane, Friday at the meeting can you wear a cup-less lace bra. (The Professor holds and rubs Jane's hand with a kind of sticky gel which smells like sperm while asking what seems to be a very personal question). Like the one you have on now. It's super (Jane's starts to get a little dizzy) sexy.

Yeah, yeah, sure... Ooooh... (Jane replies with a puzzled naive look on her face, as she starts falls into the dream-state. Unbeknownst to Jane, Yaoi is putting her into a trance with a **Love-Potion**® [22.8.2] Spermy gel substance) Professor, huh! Are you hitting on me? Ooooh... I'm dizzy...

You're a very sexy young lady Jane. Mwah... (Yaoi continues to rub the potion gel into Jane's palm). Yes, Jane I'm hitting on you. Is it okay Jane? Mwah...

Mwah... Yes of course Professor. I'll have sex with you. Huh! Huh, huh, huh... (Jane panting heavily is over-cum by the potion and instinctively drops her skirt in preparation for love-making). Mwah... I want sex!

Sex! Yes of course you want sex Jane. Tell me about the sex, will you have sex with me Jane? (Jane falls into the arms of Yaoi in a semi-consciousness state).

Yes Prof Yaoi, sex, I like sex, I want sex, I need sex. Ahhh...

Yes, Jane sex with me. This is the **Bonobo-Way** [22.19]. It is called love-making. What do you want to do Jane? Tell me.

I want love making. Peace and harmony through sex.

Peace through Sex

Yes Jane. Mwah… This is the **Bonobo-Way**® [22.19] Who Jane? Who will you have sex with, me Jane? I am your new Lordess? Mwah…

Mwah… With you Prof **Yaoi**, I want peace and love with you. Ahhh… Ahhh… (Jane is squirting out Jizzie loads as she incoherently mumbles her responses). Ahhh…

Mwah… Yes, this is right Jane! You want to (Jane is squirting into her nearly bursting Clit-Sock). Please make Bonobo love with me. Now go back to Mary. Mwah…

Mwah… Yes Prof Yaoi.

Go to Mary, because you're **Sissy-Promised** [6.B] to Mary and she loves you too Jane. Mwah…

Mwah… Yes Prof Yaoi, Mary loves me! Ahhhh…

Jane you love both Mary and I. Who do you love Jane? Mwah…

Mwah… I love you and Mary (Their both having a wet and sloppy making-out session while uttering their responses). Mwah… Yeah… Mwah…

Yes Jane, you're a ***bitch-in-heat***. Go to Mary now and hump your lover. Show her you love her! Mary owns you, she is your DOM. Go make love to her. Mwah…

Mwah… Yes Professor Yaoi (Under the influence of the hallucinogenic Love-Potion Jane agrees with the Professors every cum-mand). Mwah… Ummm… Go my little Bitch! Go to your lover! Go to Mary! (Yaoi gives Jane a strong spank on the ass and scoots her in the direction of Mary who is waiting for her down the hall from the office). Thanks for waiting Mary! (Yaoi shouts).

[1.16] WANDERING

Jane! Jane! Over here! (Jane aimlessly wanders off course). Where you going? Over here!

Mare! (Bleary eyed Jane follows the familiar voice).

Over here! Wow Jane, we're in Gurlfriend! We're in the NSA! Isn't it wonderful? Scholarships! Jane, I'm getting a sore cunt just thinking about an audience of men up my lovehole. Jane? Jane? Hey did you even here what I just said? Jane? Hello!

Yeah, Whooo! Wow! Mare! Ahhh… (Jane exhausted falls into Mary's arms). Sorry I got a little dizzy. Hmmm….

Are you feeling alright Gurlfriend?

Yeah... yeah... am good. What did you say?

The NSA offer, isn't it cool?

Yeah... yeah... Aaaah... Yeah, NSA. Sorry, yeah! Are you kidding? I squirted when she made the offer to us! It's totally cool! Did I speak with Yaoi?

Huh! Yeah, you spoke to her. (Mary wonders why Jane isn't coherent). Whoa! Jane your Clit-Sock® is way too full? Yeah, you and she were talking for a short while.

Oh Mare! Yeah, it's kinda full isn't it? I had so many orgasms in class. And then I got dizzy and, I got no idea after that!

Well here, sit down and relax. Yeah me too, I was constantly popping off in class.

Mare, when the class applauded me I squirted and then again after they applauded you, and just now with the Professors proposal.

Well Sweetheart, I got a lot in mine too let's swap socks?

Okay! I love swallowing your sweet Jizzzies. (The Gurls both unstrapped their drooping from the weight socks). Snap! Here's my sock. Snap! Here is mine.

Hmmm… Here you go! Gulp... Gulp... Yummy! (They both swallow each other's Sissy-Cream). Delicious!

Hmmm… **Jane**. (Gulping and licking sounds). Gulp! Yummy, yummy! God-of-Cocks. I love your cum taste Mare! Hmmm… I want to sleep with my head between your legs with your Clit in my mouth tonight.

Sure! Mwah… We sleep sixty-nine position a lot. Aaaagh… Gulp! It tastes so good!

Hump.... Hump... Hump... (Jane starts dry humping Mary's leg like a horny dog and pops out a load onto Mary's shapely stocking clad leg). Agh! Yeah! I Love you Mary! I love you baby! Huh! Huh! Huh! (She pants).

[1.17] TRANCE

Jane is still under Yaoi's love-making trance...

Whoa! JANE! God-of-Cocks! Calm down Gurlfriend! (Jane is still involuntarily humping Mary). What the hell are you humping me for?

Huh! Huh! Huh! I don't know! (Jane shouts).

Are you that horny you can't wait till we get home? Geeeez... You're *in-heat* Sissy-Puss! Just calm down Gurl. Jane! What's cum over you Baby?

Huh! Huh! Huh! Aghhhh... (Jane squirts off another one). Wow! I'm sorry Mary! I just got this hot flash and wanted to mount you. Aghhh, I don't know what made me act this way. I must be losing it!

Jane! Cum here (Mary hugs her lover). Wow! You're the hottest chick I ever made it with, Jane. But I've never seen you horny enough to jump-me and hump me in public.

Sorry Mare! (Jane feels insecure and hugs Mary tight). I lost track of time and I'm acting weird! What's wrong with me?

Oh Baby! I don't know. Are you okay?

Yeah, yeah... I'm fine, I think? Guess I just got over cum by my horniness for you.

Oh Jane, look what you did? You squirted **Sissy-Cream**® all over my new silk blouse.

Sorry Mare. Mwah...

Mwah… Its okay Sugar-Puss, I'll just get it dry-cleaned. I love you and understand you're a B-Type Gurl. So I guess sexual aggressiveness is to be expected.

I pop a lot! (Jane shrugs her shoulders).

Yeah! An under-statement. Jane you pop Jizzies for anything! And your Clit-Sock® has to have at least a pint in it. (Down the hatch it goes). Gulp! Gulp! (Mary drinks-down Jane's sock).

I'm a Jizz factory Mary and I LOVE IT! I'm a SISSY! (Jane shouts out loud making other students questionably look-on) And I love being a SISSY!

Gurlfriend me too. Kiss... Kissss... Mwah…

Hey! What do you say we celebrate tonight by getting some hardcore sex training at a campus Whoring-Station?

Sure Mary! Sounds good. I'll do anything as long as I'm with you Lover! Hmmm... Kiss... As long as we're kissing each other while we're getting pounded. Hmmm… (The Gurls engage in a loving embrace). Mwah…

Jane, you're my **Wildflower** [5.E1.1] Lover! Never let go Baby!

I won't Mare. Kissss… Mwah…

[1.18] CAFETERIA

The FUCIT Sissy food distribution system…

Wow Jane! This is the same thing that happens to us every time we graduate and move on to a new school. The penises always seem bigger as we go up a level in education. I guess we're growing-up?

I hear you, life-partner. The appendages are huge here! Whoa! And their nut-sacks are enormous! These are big boys!

Yeah! It seems like all the college Studs have a third leg at least all of the ones we've seen so far. They're Horse-Cocks!

Yep! I would say the men here are all perfect specimens, they're all three **H**, (3H), Hard, Hang and Horny. Well we'll definitely be getting plenty of nutritional sperm out of these big cum-hoses!

[1.19] GURLS

The Gurls meet old friends at FUCIT...

Hey Jane, look over there, it's Nicky and Tina. Hey! Nicky! Hey! Gurls! (Mary shouts).

Hey Gurls, (Jane, Mary, Nicky and Tina all hug and wet-kiss while they do a Sissy-handshake, which requires all of them to grab and squeeze each other's erect Sissy-Clits). Wow! Good to see you Gurls!

Yeah! Hey, longtime no see! Wow, we all made it to college. Whoohooo! (The Gurls all throw their hands in the air).

Have you Gurls seen any of the old **Scouting**© [16] gang here? (Tina being a Bitch doesn't reply, she just obediently goes under Nicky's skirt to suckle on her DOMs clit). Tina, where'd you go?

Nah! Well, you know some of them didn't do so hot on their college entrance exams. (Nicky replies).

What do mean Nicky?

Well, for example Tina here failed miserably. My Dad had to pay-off the test Proctor. (Nicky, to make a disciplinary point, grabs Tina by the hair and forcefully rubs her face into her cunt). Eat-me Bitch, you owe me!

Wow! Okay bribery, cool!

Right, right. Back in the Fascist days of the old USA, hundreds of years ago, after Donald (the douche-bag) Trump did his famous Quid-Pro-Quo, Cunt-gress legalized bribery.

Yep! There're laws legalizing, bribery, pay-offs, extortion, ransoms for government officials. It's all part of the Modern Social Economic System, the **MSES** [4.D-G2.1].

Tssss.... Yeah, but Mary at a cost. My Dad will never forgive me. As part of the pay-off he ended up taking a proctology exam up his ass by the test Proctor. So now I own this expensive Bitch!

Yeah, yeah... Well, the modern Special Integration School System, the SISS® tests are quite rigorous. The Sexual Aptitude Test, the **SAT** [11.K.5] challenges the sexual skills needed in the MSES.

Wow! Well I assumed all us Sissy-Gurls from the preschool and Scouts were doing alright!

Well Mary, college isn't for everyone.

True and Jane and I didn't real stay in touch much because most of them went to the other Integration Schools in different districts. I mean other than an occasional Weee-Chat message or two and a Cum-munity sponsored recreational Sissy-Sex® festival or **Fuckfest**® once in a while.

Well yeah, yeah… But still they did alright I guess even if they didn't go to college. Like for example, **Dana** and **Lisa** (EN08) went into the military and joined the US Army Sissy Corp.

Ooooh my Cock-God! That's sooo cool!

Yeah, yeah! And **Martha** (EN09) talked to them and found out they both signed-up for a tour of duty on Mars.

Wow! Mars! Wait! Doesn't the Eurasian Union own the Red planet?

Yeah, but since the new treaties with the Eurasian Union we're graciously allowed to have a small research stations on Mars now. So they volunteered for their first Fucked-Out Mission, **FOM** [25.38].

Ummm! Those are dangerous assignments. Aren't the Sissies utilized to provide labor compensation transactions (LCT) and utility-sex for the servicemen?

Ah huh! They send them on a **FOM** to the remote bases on the frontier of the Red Planet is carried out to service all the horny servicemen in need of compensation.

Nicky, it sounds like fun to me! Granted I bet the Non-Stud grunt enlisted Soldiers work em hard, I could imagine how sore their cunts get! (Jane chimes in enthusiastically, while rubbing her twat).

Yeah Jane, but those two are tough for sure! They're both tomboy types. And after they volunteered for the mission, the military did the, Pussy Blooming Procedure, the **PBP** [4.D-G1.1] on both of them.

Wow! They got Rosebudded! Holy Sissy-Poop®. Hardcore!

Yeah well the military doesn't fuck-around. They were having problems with Sissies getting **Vaganus®** injuries doing constant FO® so now they just Rosebud® all the Sissies prior to going to the frontiers.

Hey, this is modern life in Sissydom®. Face it! Gurls like us do a lot of the hard jobs in creating a more non-violent Human-Sissy® culture.

Truly put Mary. Oh! And **Jean** and **Martha** (EN09) eloped.

Huh! Wow! I feel like I've been living under a rock. This is real news!

Yeah, yeah… They got DOM-Bitch Marriage, **DBM®** [6.B.8].

Holy-Cock! That's awesome!

Ooh yeah! Their parents were in shock but the Gurls are happy. Jean's Dad gave them some money to start a **SissyWear®** [10.2.1] shop business in Peniston New Jerksey [44.5] near the university. And I heard sales are doing great.

Ooooh Nicky, I'm so happy for them! (The Gurls hug). Mwah…

Then there's **Jennifer**!

Oh what's happening with her? More, more tell us more!

Well that Sissy-Gurl® met a really nice sophisticated well-to-do Sissy-Family Lady, Judy. And now Jenifer lives with her Sissy Breeding Girl-Bitch®. The Sissy Breeding-Marriage, an **SBM** [6.E] wedding is planned to happen during winter break. And I'm sure all of us from the old gang will be invited.

Well it's so nice, I'm glad for her too. Ha haaa... Jane and I have lead pretty mundane lives compared to all these other Gurls!

Oh, oooh... Wait! And word has it Jenifer has already knocked-up her human bitch Judy!

Hoo... Hooo! Wow! Pre-marital pregnancy, cool!

Yeah so don't tell anybody.

Oh, and Annie? Where did that little nympho tramp end up? (Mary has always held a grudge against Annie for having played around with Jane so much).

Oh well, yeah Annie. Aaaah... She kinda disappeared (Nicky says in a regrettable tone).

WHAT? Whatta mean?

Well Jane, you know Annie had a hard-time with her parents. She always had bruises? Everybody knew she had problems at home.

Yeah, yeah... She would have bruises, which she always claimed were from bumping into things. I kinda had an idea things weren't so right with her and her folks.

Well, I guess she left town.

Where did she go? Or why did she go? She could have just gone to the Police and turned in her parents in for abuse if they beat her! Sniff... Snifff...

Well, Jean said she saw her walking into a Whoring-Station near a FEMA camp and she looked kind of scanky. So, I assume the poor Sissy-Gurl is just working as a common Hoe at a **C-Type** Station.

Dam! I liked Annie soooo much. It's a shame! Her idiot parents did this to her! (Jane shouts). Sniff... Sniff...

Well, yeah Jane, you and Annie were always tight at **JAS**® camp, but I guess this is what happens to a Sissy-Gurl if you grow-up getting smacked around by your human parent's. You just become a common Hoe, working at a C-Type Station.

Oooh, a real travesty of American life! Sniff... Sniff... It makes me so sad (Mary sniffles and puts her arm around Jane). It's okay Jane. Mwah...

Yeah me too, I'm sorry for her. Annie was always a lot of fun, lots of energy, playful and great in bed! I spent a few nights in her bunk, really hot sex. Sniff... Sniff...

Tammy? (EN08) Have you heard from her?

Oh! That's a hell of a story! Her **Stud**® Daddy is a lawyer and has connections in Washingcum. So he got her into the National Sissy University in the District of **Cunt-cumbia**, DC. And she has a student job working for a Sissy Senator on Capitol Hill.

Wow! Tammy is really something! So smart and charismatic!

Yeah she said she's majoring in Law.

Awesome! She was always the loudest in the group. She'll make a great lawyer with that big mouth of hers. And she's the only African-American Sissy I know.

Yeah! Well most African-Americans, for good reasons, relocated to the African-Union, the **AU** [22.30] after the thirteenth Amendment [17.13] in the Second Cunt-Stitution declared all Caucasian-White, Non-Stud, wage-earning, working citizens were debt-slaves.

Right, right... And then the AU countered with the Soft Black-Supremacy, the **SBS** [22.28]. They legalized White slaves on the African continent as a sanction against the USA Inc.

And rightfully so!

Right! What goes around, cums around!

Oh hey Mary, talking about government stuff, I heard about your nomination for class president and I just wanted you to know I'll vote for you and I'm sure Tina would if Bitches could vote.

Well thanks. Okay! Gurls hey, we're hungry, you're hungry, let's all get together for studying or to just hang-out and share some body fluids.

Yeah, yeah... I got your cell number and WeeChat. Okay, later Gurls. Kissss... Kiss... (They do the Sissy-Shake & jerk of each other's clits as they say goodbye) Kisss... Mwah... Love you!

Slap, TINA! Stop suckling my Cocklette Bitch! (Nicky yanks hard on Tina's leash) Say goodbye to Mary and Jane. (Tina is in tears from her being slapped, as DOM Nicky shakes her head disapprovingly). You ingrateful little Bitch!

Bye Jane! Bye Mary! Kisss... See you Gurls. (From the excitement of saying goodbye, all their Gurly-Clits are profusely squirting streams of Jizzzies into their Clit-Socks).

Cum on Tina!

Ouch! Ow! (Nicky yanks hard on Tina's leach). Slam! Yank!

Huh! (Mary and Jane are just standing there, in the busy cafeteria, shaking their heads in disbelief as Nicky practically drags Tina by her leash to a lunch Milking-Station line).

[1.20] CULTURE

Good seeing Tina and Nicky again? (Mary says with a stunned look on her face). Huh! Wow.

Yeah, let's stay in touch with them and keep an eye open to whether Tina is in danger!

Oh definitely. Those two are a train-wreck waiting to happen. Nicky is way, way too rough with her (Mary shakes her head in disapproval). Tssss… I'm just glad I didn't turn-out to be as mean as Nicky.

Mwah… Me too **Mare**. Huh! As promiscuous as I am, if you were mean as her, you woulda beat the crap out of me by now. Mwah… I love Mare!

Love you too Sweetheart. Mwah…

And hey! I know you'll get elected class president. You've always been elected class president in every school we've attended, Mare.

Yeah Babe, who knows maybe I'll go into politics and be cum a Senator or Cunt-gresswomen someday. All the Senators are members of the National Sissydom Association, the **NSA** [4.D-G6.13].

Oh! **Mare**, I want to be your political whore and get the votes for you with my pussy! After all, I'm your slut Gurlfriend! Mwah...

Oh sweetheart, I adore you Honey! Hmm... Kisss...

Hey! So you were sharing with me your observations about the huge penises here at FUCIT?

Well yeah! The boys here have to be from a **Stud**® [1.A1.1] Family. After all FUCIT is part of the Sissy-Stud Integration Education System. Students are here to be integrated into Americas Super Sissy-Stud Culture of the future.

Yeah Mary, they have to be from a Stud-Family® for admission to the university and I hear the Admissions office is very selective about their sizes, regardless of their school grades. This would explain why they're all hang-like-horses.

Hey, I don't care how big it is, horse-cock or Sissy-Clit, I'm hungry for Dick-Milk. Let's swallow some Man-Cream®.

I hear you, I'm hungry! And checkout the feeding system, it's different here.

Wow! Yeah, it's way different than Integration high school. The Feeders get their pricks prepped prior to offering their cum-hoses to our hungry mouths by a high-tech sucking machine which stops sucking when it senses the dick is ready to pop a load.

Cool! AI automation. This means we have to do less work for the same amount of **Dick-Milk®**.

Yeah, awesome! For our bottoms as well. The Stud-Boys are prepped by machines prior to penetration. And it only takes a few pokes at our love tunnels for them to pop their Jizzie load into our eagerly waiting cum-buckets. This is too good to be true!

Hey! We live in the best Cunt-tree in the world. Only in America can this many highly educated people share their body fluids freely and not be arrested for sodomy or rape or indecent exposer, or immoral crap!

Yep! Well, this is the United States of America Incorporated our society is more advanced. Our integration schools are so well orgasmized and have the latest Sissy® support equipment.

Sure Jane, FUCIT has 69,000 students here so it has to be fast to be able to service this many aroused men.

Right, right… And there're only a few hundred Pure Sissies attending, so it means each Sissy has to take at least several hundred loads per day?

Wow! That's why it's so fast and orgasmized.

Oh yeah! We get boys in both ends for a reason! I love college!

Well, it's setup just like a real production Whoring-Station. And I guess we might as well get used to it. Because this is what we'll be doing after graduating from college.

Yeah Jane, but only for the first year because we're Pure Breed Sissies, **PBS®** and plus we'll have Sissyology degrees. If we take our Certification exam, we'll both be **CSW** [2.B2.5]. This means we'll probably get promoted to management or be assigned to a, L-Type **WS** [7.G4]. We'll be servicing a more select group of Studs with more benefits because of their larger penis sizes and stature in the Stud-Sissy® Cum-munity.

Heck! Maybe we'll work in a **WSL**? But regardless, please remember my little Wildflower® we'll always have each other. Kiss... Mwah... (Hugs). Jane, look on my tablet the table for Whoring-Station types and the **L-Type** [7.G4.L] is the best.

Yeah, yeah... Great Mary! We'll be servicing bigger high-class pricks. But for right now, let's just find two benches because I'm having a real need to be filled at both ends. Mwah...

Mwah... Sure Jane, I'm just glad they give us a two hour lunch break. This way we can get undressed, put our stuff in our lockers, get both our holes filled and it leaves plenty of time to douche-out, do a **PrettyPuss**® test and do our hair and make-up then get dressed again before having to get to class.

Hah, ha... Yada, yada, ya... Yeah Mary, You know I never wear make-up and I'd be naked if there wasn't a dress code at FUCIT.

[1.21] SAR

Note: skip this part if you hate mushy, tearjerker stuff...

Oooh Jane Honey, you know I'm a classic Sissy DOM, and Gurls like me require some extra time to get prettied up. You Bitch® types who have a sexual activity rank (SAR) of Wildflower® are just like wild weeds. All of you Sissies with your rank have the highest Cockage® totals and you screw anyone, anywhere, anytime. But Jane, you know what?

What Boss? Burrrr… I just got a chill. Hmmm… Why do I feel like you're gonna deliberate a cold sobering speech to me?

Well Jane, most of the Hoe Gurls who work at C-Type Whoring-Stations are Wildflower® Bitches? **Wildflowers** [5] like you Jane!

So! Mare, what are you getting at? (Jane answers with a puzzled look on her face).

Do you want to end up like Annie? (Mary be cums overly bearing on Jane).

Cum on Mary! What are you trying to say?

Working as a Hoe in a C-Station? Just like that scanky little tramp you used to play with at JAS® camp behind my back. Now that little cunt is nothing but a common Hoe! Is that what you want Jane? Do you want to end-up like Annie? She's nothing more than a working class Whore!

Huh! Wow! (Jane is stunned my Mary's attitude). Yeah! You know, you're right Mary. I'm just a piece-of-shit Wildflower®. Sniff… Sniff…. I don't deserve to be your Bitch®. Sniff…. We can be cum a Nicky and Tina pair.

Jane! Look! (Mary forcefully grabs Jane's arm firmly and looks at her sternly). If we're going to be cum life-partners and get married you have to realize and except, I'm not like you. We have different **SAR**® scores. Jane I'm just a Trap®.

Hey! I'm faithful to you Mare! I don't play with other DOM® ladies! I don't care what your rating is!

Yeah I know. But I've only had about 60,000 **LCT**® penetrations! And Conservative Sexy DOM Ladies like me be cum Senators, lawyers, doctors, directors, administrators. We're always going to need much more time to pretty-up our sexy smart Sissy selves.

Okay wait a second. Where are you going with this? And why are you so even bothering to be concerned about a silly ranking?

Jane let's face it. I'll never have as high a Cockage® total as you. In fact it's an embarrassment for a DOM to have a higher score than her Bitch®.

Hello! Pssss… I'm not counting! Calm down Mare, you're making a mountain out of a molehill.

Jane, all I'm trying to say is, (Jane knows Mary has some weird self-esteem issues about quantity of love-making). Jane, look at me Sweetheart! If I'm gonna have a successful career I can't be like you!

Mary! Tssss… I know and hey, I love you! I'll never try to change you. I Love you because you're a hot sexy Lady. And besides, I don't think I would be compatible with another Wildflower like Annie. I love what we have between us.

Okay! Sniff... Jane... Sniff... But I just get these feelings sometimes! Like, you think I'm not going to keep up with you. Sniff... And, and, and you'll break-off our Sissy-Promise. Huh, hah, ha…. (Mary is balling her eyes out for some not yet known reason).

What? No way Mary! Are you kidding? I'm promised to you and I meant every word when I took my Sissy-Promise vows with you. Mwah… You're the one for me.

You sure? Huh, hah, ha…. (Tears still flowing).

YES…!!!... I love you forever! Nothing is gonna change this. I've loved you since our scheming Mother's put us in the same baby crib to suckle each other's clits. I'm the one you should be worrying about losing. Not the other way around, Mare.

Jane this is (Tears rolling down Mary's cheeks) never sniff... **go**... sniff... **ing**... sniff... **to**... sniff... **happen**! Huh, hah…

Sure Mary. Hey, I know how you feel. I mean, we've been in love with each other since before preschool. But, you grew-up and became a beautiful, refined, classy, mature and sophisticated Sissy DOM® Lady. And I'm just a Wildflower, a little Bitch® who never grew-up! I'm a scank tramp compared to you!

Jane, we've been together forever! And I don't want you calling yourself a scank.

Yeah! But face it. I'm a **B-Type** [1.A2.2] which was designed in a laboratory to be sexually abused by men. Mary you're a **D-Type** [1.A2.1] and you were designed to control pathetic little misbehaving Gurls like me. Those are our stations in life, in the MSES. It's simple, I'm the worker bee and you're the queen! And just like Annie, I'm a working class **Whore**®.

Stop it Jane! Just stop it! It's not who we are. We're not Nicky and Tina (Meeting their old friends in the Cafeteria kinda frightened Mary about the future of her relationship with Jane).

Right! We're different, in a good way. And NO! I'm not refined like you Mary. I never wear a pretty dress or fine lingerie, sexy garter-belts with silky and lace, fancy push-up bras or put on make-up or Gurly perfume with jewelry like you.

Huh! And you're okay with that?

Yeah Mare! I spit, swear and fuck! And get into trouble! I'm always the one the Stud® boys want to bounce up and down while they slap me around. Those boys constantly screw me because, to a Stud® I'm just a common Hoe they can legally abuse.

I don't like the way men handle you, Jane. Snifff… Snifff…

Snifff… Snifff… Jizz-Us® now you got me crying. Snifff… Snifff… Look, you're the one who always cums to my rescue to pick me up after the Stud® boys are done with me at a gangbang party.

I'll always be there for you, Jane. Snifff…

Snifff… Yeah, I know. You're the one with class. Me and you we're like, Lady-and-the-Tramp. Haaa haa… You're the DOM Lady in the top one percent of our economy. I'm the working class Tramp at the bottom!

Oh Jane, stop it! You know I would never think less of you regardless of what you wear or do or whatever. Sniffle… sniffle.

Hmmm… In reality, I'll graduate college like you Mary but unlike you, I'll probably spend the rest of my life working in a C Station like my un-educated, not breed from birth, transitioned **SIT**® [1.4] Daddy.

NO! We'll always be together **Jane**!

Yeah, dreams cum true. But face it. You'll probably have a very prestigious job as an executive in some big high raise office building in the city. Or like you said, maybe have a political career in Washingcum.

Stop it! Snifff... Snifff...

You'll always have your game on, **Mary**. Always have upward social and career mobility. Me, like I said, I'll always look like a scanky little seven year old child and be an object who low in cum, working class Non-Stud men abuse. I'll never attract handsome **Stud**® men to me like you do.

Hey, (Mary grabs Jane by the shoulders with both hands, looks her straight in the eyes). You're not just a Wildflower® you're my Wildflower! And nobody else's! (Rivers of tears flowing).

DO YOU UNDERSTAND ME!

Yeah, yeah... Take it easy. (Jane is just trying to be appeasing to Mary in hopes of calm down her rants). And there's nothing wrong with being a well-loved, DOM owned scank. Mwah...

I don't care what Sissy-breeding **Girl-Bitch**® the government assigns you as a Breeding wife! I don't care where you work or what kind of job you have, or what type of men you attract. I will (After witnessing the Nicky-Tina incident, Mary is having a break-down with just the thought of losing Jane).

Oh! **Mare**, Lover, calm down. Mwah...

I'll always, sniffle... sniffle... sniffle... be... sniffle... there for sniffle... you! I'm yours and you're mine! And in my heart this will never change Jane. Sniffle.... Sniffle...

Okay Mary, promise? (The Gurls hug each other in a tight embrace).

Yes, yes, I promise and am promised to you only. Sniffle... Sniffle.

But promise me one more thing sexy DOM Lady? (Mary looks at Jane with a puzzled look on her face). Promise me you'll give me a good spanking tonight before bed?

Ooooh! My dear precious Jane. Mwah... I will do anything you want me to, my sweet little Wildflower®. (Mary plays the mommy role and pinches Jane's cheek) Kiss.... But we got one more class today, let's go get an education? Mwah...

Okay! But don't let go of my hand Lady. Mwah...

Oh Jane sweetheart! I'll never let go of you my precious Lover.

End of the mushy part...

[1.22] GOSSIP

Mary & Jane entering the classroom...

Look its **Mary**. (Says a Stud® student while the Gurls pass by).

Oh yeah it's Mary, Mary Dune and her Bitch **Jane** something.

Yeah you're right. Wow! Mary's in this class too. Cool! The video taken of her and her Bitch in Sissyology class went viral! Here it is on **SissyTube**®. (The dude shows it on his tablet).

Oh Cool! Yeah it should be a great class with Mary in it, let's try to sit near her (The guys stare with open mouths in awe of Mary's beauty as she passes them by).

Sure, sure and I heard Mary was nominated for class president.

Ahhh… She'll win for sure just on her looks alone. And her hot knockout body of hers, WOW! And hey, she had the highest college entrance exam score too. She got a 1600 on the **SAT**® [11.K.5] with a 200 plus IQ.

Dam! She's smart and beautiful! And she's won beauty contests against **Stud**® females!

Right, right… Mary has brains and beauty but the slut Jane, what's up with that?

Oh yeah! The scrawny little cunt follows Mary around wherever she goes. And check-it-out, she's not even on a leash! Worst, the way she dresses, like a common Hoe! The cup-less bra? What's that about and she ain't got no tits!

Huh! Yeah straight out of a Japanese Hentai cartoon. And Dude, it looks like she's got a pint hanging from her **Clit-Sock**®.

Well, the word is, Jane **Bitch**® is just a dirty Hoe Bag.

Really? What's the story?

Ooooh! She's a big time Hoe! I heard back in high school everybody screwed her including the Non-Stud janitors!

Uoooh! Scank!

Yeah and a gang of Sissy **Mutts**® used to beat the crap out of her regularly for mooching on their stable of Studs.

Wow a real tramp. So, I wonder why Mary has this wild little sex toy, Hoe as her Bitch?

No idea, considering how fine Mary is, she can have a harem of Bitches but she only keeps this one little scank around. I mean she could obviously have any **Bitch**® she wants.

Yeah it's kinda weird!

I don't know but beyond that brother, my uncles a cop up in MO-Town where Mary and Jane are from. And he said he raided this illegal Non-Stud (NS) Gentlemens club onetime. They arrested about three hundred NS assholes. Then imagine this, he found Jane the Hoe lying there on the floor, exhausted in a puddle of NS cum wads.

Ooooh! Ugh! Dude! Ahhhh… Gross! What a promiscuous little fuckhole she is! Non-Stud (NS) Jizz? Ugh! I'm gonna barf!

Oh yeah! She's a real low-class cum-bucket, nothing but a Cock-Toilet. Even worst she was filled and covered with Non-Stud Jizz. Totally fucked-out of her mind.

Shhhh…it! Man, I beat Jane is a **Cockoholic** [7.G5.2]. What a waste of perfectly good Sissy cunt.

Yeah, I'm never sticking my dick in that Hoe, she's real trash. She probably has all kinds of deceases from Non-Studs.

Right but Mary, she's a really fine classy Lady? She's just strutting around in a Sissy Lady Power-Suite, Holy-Poop! I took one look at her and was like, Wow!

Get the fuck out of her way… !!!…

Yeah, yeah… She's first-class and the finest piece-of-ass at FUCIT. I'd like to get a date with her.

Oh yeah! Mary's a choice kinda **Gurl**® she looks so fine. Dam! Look at those massive tits!

She's a real foxy Lady, puts most human female girls to shame.

Well hey! If she gives us a cold shoulder, we can always bang her in their dorm **Whorehouse**®. Its number, WH069S.

The Gurls are used to boys ogling at them…

Jane? What the hell are they pointing at us for?

I have no clue Mary or care. Let's just ignore them and get seats in the front row.

Yeah, good idea. I wanna be able to wink at the Professor Lady. **Rimme** is a department head.

Chapter: 2 College Part B

[2.1] RIMME

Sex Psychology...

My name is Professor **Rimme** and I'm your instructor, mentor and the Head of the Sissyology Department. This is Sex Psychology 101. You will be introduced to the parts of psychology which explores why we humans desire to have sex with a particular type of livestock called Sissy. I'm proud to announce your school, The Federal University of Cultural Integration and Transition, **FUCIT**, is part of a nationwide program for research into this fascinating topic. It's called ISIS, the Institute for the Study of Intercourse with Sissies, (ISIS).

This topic focuses on the transition of all Americans into an integrated, homogeneous Sissy and Stud culture. First, I'll just breeze over the history which lead-up to our sex-based culture here in the USA Inc.

This was all started back in the year 2213 after the overthrow of the Fascist American government. Then the Second United States **Cunt-Stitution** [17] was partially ratified yet passed into law. Afterward the Sissification® Act was voted down by Cunt-gress. The Cunt-gress members who voted it down were all immediately Imp-Eached. Then to expedite the passing of the Sissification® Act, the power of the President of the United States Incorporated was implemented to enact it by law by an Executive Order. So this was the will of the people! This is in accordance with our newly formed, Supreme Imperial Executive branch of government. This was a major improvement over our previous Democratic government. Now our President has the

Imperial power to impose his will for the good of all of us, as Clitcum, Boosh, O-Bomb and Trump had in the past, called the **CBOT** Era [21.B.5].

But you know all this and I won't bore you with politics. So let's move on to a more exciting part of Psychology, SEX! Ok, you all look shocked about my abruptness. So, I'll ask a question. Who here likes sex? Raise your hand if you do. Okay, so everyone raised their hands, I think if you didn't please just leave this lecture hall.

Ho! Hah! Haaaa haaa haa… (The whole class breaks out in laughter). Haaa, haa, ha…

Yes, this would be funny and really weird too, if any of you didn't like sex!

Here's another one of my weird multi-part questions which you should be used too by the end of the semester. (1) How can someone have a big dick and at the same time be a Sissy and if so (2) would this girlified person be gay because of their super long appendage? Oooh! (All the students have a blank stare). This is a tough one. Okay, no hands. Hmmm… Tough room!

Oooh! Sorry, there is one hand up, go ahead, the Stud-looking gentlemen in the middle row.

Professor, I'm a little confused by your question. Can the person be breed from birth as a Sissy and then want to be a man with a big penis? You know what I'm saying, like Transgender person?

This is a very good question. The answer is no. **BfB**® purebreds are biologically through gene manipulation, brought into this world as females with a micropenis, **Vaganus**® and believe it or not a uterus, which is inoperable for some weird biological reason. Although there is research being conducted at Johns **Hopkinky**® Hospital [22.33] to activate the dormant Sissy-Uterus®. And you cannot reverse the effects of gene re-engineering which created them. They're Homo-Sis-Sapiens and can't change biology. Basically they're monkeys who look like humans.

But I wanted an answer to my question! Let me be more specific. I'm focusing on one of the hottest and most misunderstood topics in all of **Sissydom**®. And we're gonna spend a lot of time on the topic of Sissies and the different types of Sissies this semester.

[2.1] SIDE-NOTE

And before we get into this part of the lecture I need to go over some basic facts and theories about breeding Sissies. (1) In the USA Inc. currently Sissies are brought into this world by way of an inoculated Human-Human (HH) host couple, where both parents are human. But there are historical and archaeological studies which have linked the breeding of Vaganus® through the millenniums.

Ooooh! Wow, Ohhh… (The entire auditorium is clamoring over the thought of two different Genomes breed together). Can they do that Professor?

Yes, yes, the researchers have linked, but yet to prove the **Sissy**® creature has existed for thousands possibly millions of years. They were isolated from the masses kept in cages and confined in the caves, castles and cathedrals of the warlords, kings, queens, royalty and deities of the church. They were simply used as sex toys by these powers.

So (2) the **Vaganus**® can be breed with a Sissy-Human (SH) couple where the human female is inoculated to breed with the Sissy-Gurl®. And there's studies being conducted at **Hardon-Vard**® which has proven, due to the lack of contrary evidence, that all of the emperors, cum-manders, royalty, prime ministers, presidents, Popes, heads-of-state, leaders of the world are all breed from a SH pair of parents.

Wow, Ahhhh… Wow, Ohhh… Ooooh (The class is in disbelief). You sure Professor? Ohhh… (Grumbling in the lecture hall).

Oh! And guess what the children breed from the SH parents turns out to be… (Rimme pauses the answer to create a cliff hanger).

What? What? (The students are in suspense about the answer).

Wait I haven't got to this part yet!

Ahhhh! Professor! Give us the answer! Ahhh! (Students are at the edge of their seats with anticipation).

[2.3] HOMO-FEMININUS

Okay! With that side-note out of the way. One of the most compelling types of Sissies to learn about is, as I've mentioned, Sissies with large penises. These humanoids born with this anomaly are creatures breed to be feminine, by loving, Sissification drug altered, doped-up, Sissy parents. These parents both have long Sissy-Lineage® in their families so needless to say all the males in their families had extremely small micro-dicks. But in the case of the **Homo-Femininus**® [18.2] the Sissy child is born with an unusually long penis with huge testicles.

Wow! Huh! Oooh! Is that possible? You wouldn't lie to us, would you professor? Huh! How big? Whoa! It's freaky!

And folks! Calm down! I'm talking BIG here! Longer than any **Stud**® penis on record and in most cases being sixteen inches or longer when fully erect. When soft it reaches half way down to their knee caps of the Sissy when soft. (Rimme, to make her point, grabs a piece of chalk and scribbles an exaggeratingly long penis on the board).

Oh! My Cock-God! Wow! Huh! (The students are all taken aback by the Professors claim). How can that be Professor?

Well, I understand how inconceivable you might find this. This is definitely one of the most bazar and fascinating topics in all of Sissydom®. But strangely enough it also is the one which has the least amount of data compiled about it. This is mostly due to the fact, these half-woman, half-man type mutated freaks are extremely secretive about their lives. Very little is known about these weird Sissy abominations.

There're even myths, old wives-tale, legends passed down through the ages about them being hideous monsters reaping havoc across the land. Raping and torturing fragile little Sissy **B-Type**® Bitches. All of which are unsubstantiated of course. And just a note here, for all you young Stud® fellows in the class who dream of having the biggest dick in the world. The benefits of which is debatable. I mean, an extremely long penis like the one I've described can be both a burden and a blessing to the one wielding it. Hell, if not careful someone could trip over the fucking thing! It's so long! Haaa haa…

Huh! Hah... Haaa... Oooh... hoo... Aaah... Haaa, (Only the Stud students are laughing). Haaa, haaaa… you said, fucking Professor! Haaaa haaa... heee... heee.

Or worst yet, poke their eye out with a dick that big!

Hah haaa… Oooh, Hoo Aaah, Haaaa... Haa…

Okay, settle down, settle down class. Yes, I know I said the **F** word, get used to it. But enough joking around. It's obvious, I have to re-word my question or provide more historical information here. So, some of you might be wondering if someone can be both a Sissy and be Gay.

First off, we all know Gay, Man-on-Man sex or **MOM®** [4.D-G4.19] is illegal in the United States Inc. since the second USA Inc. **Cunt-Stitution** [17] was partially ratified. Although, some High-Ranking Bureaucrats can engage in Man-on-Man by simply submitting the correct form. And for that matter the acceptance of Sissydom® and human mutation is rejected and therefore illegal in every Cuntree except the United States of America Incorporated. But it's a social issue and this is a sex psychology course. So let's try to answer the question with science not politics.

Well let's start here! One fact is these freaks are a product of skewed chromosomes. This turns out a very unusual anomaly of the Hono-Sis-Sapien called **Homo-Femininus®**. And it's natural for a highly developed and socially controlled industrial nation like the USA Inc. to reject the thought that nature made a mistake. But taking a scientific approach we just have to ignore the occurrence of a Homo-Femininus® because it happens so rarely. (The students are scratching their heads about the logic).

This Homo-Femininus® phenomenon occurs in approximately one in every sixty-nine hundred thousand Sissies bred, making it extraordinarily rare. As I've mentioned the parent's oddly enough are both from normal Sissy-Breeder® families whose male members have a long-history of astonishingly small penises. But the verdict is not in as to whether the parents are predominantly HH or SH, or whatever yet.

You see! The Homo-Femininus® Sissy child is born with all of the feminine mannerisms of a normal Sissy. Feelings about her prettiness and their physical features are all female. So they're like most Sissy children, except they grow huge breasts and are larger physically height and weight wise. But there's one thing much different about them. Their Gurly-Clit grows into a penis which is much larger than children born from a **Stud**® Class family. In fact the penis of a Homo-Femininus child oftentimes grows to be twice as long as the penis of a child born from a Stud® family and this is regardless if the Stud family is taking the enlargement **PED** [4.D-G1.8] medication or not.

Yes, the cute petite long blonde haired Sissy in the cup-less bra.

Professor Rimme, if the abnormal Homo-Femininus child is born a Sissy, would they want to have sex with men like Sissies do?

Great question! And an interesting one, the answer can be broken down into two parts. Yes, the mind of the Homo-Femininus® desires to have sex with men as do all Sissies. But the penis of the Homo-Femininus wants to have sex with Sissy Gurl®. So, the answer is both yes and no. And if you're not confused yet, you will be!

And it's why we're studying this particular abnormality. Because as students majoring in Sissyology there is going to be times in your professional careers in the Whoring Industry where being familiar with these oddities of Sissydom® will be beneficial to you.

Being familiar with both the Homo-Femininus and our Compensation System developed by our Department of the Treasury and **DHMC** [4.D-G6.1], is going to be very helpful to you in dealing with Sissy-Stud issues. And oddly enough these special yet unusual Sissies play an important role in the social economic system we call the **MSES**®. [0]

Professor! I'm very confused. (**Jane** has never seen any of this stuff in her previous textbooks).

Yes, I can see why you would be confused by the topic of penis size. (Rimme gives a stern look at Jane). Because young lady you're a **Sissy**®. And are on the opposite side of the penis size spectrum in relationship to the Homo-Femininus. And especially considering you Sissies and this might sounds a bit demeaning, but realistically speaking, you have no admirable way of using your micro-size penis to give sexual pleasure to men or women. In fact the only redeeming feature of a B-Type Bitch like you is your desire to process **LCT**® [12.L1.0] with your Vaganus® like an ATM machine.

Huh! Professor! (Jane interjects).

Let me finish! And honestly, Sissies are classified by the United States Department of Agriculture as livestock animals and used primarily for processing labor compensation or for breeding. So if not used as a Whoring animal because of an abnormal sexual desire, they're often just sold by our government as pets, aka sex-toys to support the needs of the wealthy **Stud**® entre-

manures or political figures here in the USA Inc. And on a historical note. You can see the similarity between the Sissy-Class and the working middle class several hundred years ago. The Sissies will be utilized till our Government exhausts their usefulness as it had the Working Class in the post Lehman Brothers Crisis era.

Yes, you're right Professor, I'm sorry I asked, Geeeez.

Geeezz... Mary, what an asshole! (Jane whispers to Mary).

Shush Jane! Don't you dare get us in trouble with the head of the Sissyology department!

Ahhh.... My apologies to the young Sissy student who asked the question, I didn't mean to offend anyone. But so often times I do. And No please don't be sorry young lady, I'm the one who should be sorry my dear. Maybe I was too coarse with my answer.

Perhaps this can clear up some of the misconception here and get my foot out of my mouth. As you know Sissies fundamentally have a one track mind, their modus-operandi, their only method of operation, is to please men with their **Vaganus**® also inappropriately known as an, Ass-Pussy.

I mean Sissies are designed, engineered and bred to be sex machines by the United States government. And quite frankly the USA Inc. government has always enslaved its population into austerity of some kind or another under the cloak of democracy by the Uber rich aristocrats. Which is all for our benefit of course! These wealthy citizens graciously provide their resources to control our society and government for a good reason. Our government typically gets out of control and abuses its citizenry. So there needs to be oversight of the Bourgeoisie politicians.

Unfortunately this rarely control anything. But my research her at the university is funded from the government so let's just skip this part of the lesson.

So Professor, is the **B-Type** [1.A2.2] necessary?

Yes, yes, yes… Of course they are a vital part! The Sissy type worked the hardest is the **B-Type**, like the Sissy who asked the question earlier. They're worked like farm animals, like a mule in Whoring-Stations. Why you ask? Well they were bred to do so! You see class the Sissy is not a human creature as they appear to be. They were created in Sissyology laboratories here in the USA Inc. by altering their genetic traits to produce man pleasing sex objects called Homo-Sis-Sapiens who are typically referred to as, Sissies. On the flip-side of your Sissydom world is, Homo-Femininus® who are just genetic freaks who are NOT concerned about how much or if any pleasure, their **Sissy-Sex®** partner is experiencing. And their definitely not concerned with their governments profit margins.

So what we do know is this, the Homo-Femininus® is only concerned with the pleasure their long pricks are experiencing. They get horny less frequently than normal Sissies. Thank the God-of-Cocks! But still have a strong desire to ejaculate their copious amounts of **Love-Potion®** [22.8.2] onto and into their un-suspecting victims. Homo-Femininus basically is very similar in nature to the old post-Bretton Woods, interventionist, Neocon, imperialistic, fascist government of the old United States. They're devious, narcissists, greedy, conceded, arrogant, imperialistic bigots, macho, domineering, controlling, self-centered assholes who just want to enjoy pleasure and profit at the expense of others.

Whoa! Wow! Freaks! Yeah sounds bad-ass (The students are all discussing and grumbling about the revelation they just hear). Holy-Poop! What the heck! Frankenstein-ish!

[2.4] SECRETIVE

And another point I need to make. The Homo-Femininus® are very secretive by nature. Like I was saying, we know very little about this strange group of Sissies. They live lives in typical roles, usually as professionals of some kind or another, Teachers, Politicians, Sissyologists, Gene-Engineers, Sissy-Poop Culinary Masters, Professional Wrestlers, Lawyers, Proctologists and Judges. But unbeknownst to their co-workers, colleagues, neighbors and friends, if they have any, they live a secretive erotic life. And typically never bestow the knowledge of their sexual intentions, physical abnormality or social class to anyone. Instead the Homo-Femininus live solitary lives as freaks of nature under a facade of normality.

Huh! Now on to the really spooky stuff! The psychology of the Homo-Femininus Sissy mind is not normal. They rarely have sex compared to a normal Sissy. Like I said, as seldom as maybe just several times a day compared to a normal Sissy who has on the average, sixty-nine or more orgasms per day.

But when they do have a need to ejaculate and have chosen a Sissy to violate they are extremely clever and cunning about how they lure their prey into their web so they can insert their ominous looking massive voodoo-stick up into the sweet vulnerable unadulterated **Sissy-Gurl**® lovehole. And this is when they hose the precious Gurls special-place with mind controlling, psychotropic Love-Potion cream, turning the frail flowering young Sissy-Gurl into a SEX SLAVE of the Homo-Fem.

Ooooh! Wow! Ooouuugh! I'm not bending over for that! Yeah it's scary! I'm locking my dorm door tonight! (The Sissies are all squirting into their Clit-Socks, frightened by the Professors lecture).

Ok, Okay! Calm down you Sissies, you have nothing to fear. Ahhh! Calm down. God-of-Cocks© you'd think I was talking about Vampires or something.

One question Professor! (Mary raises her hand).

Yes, the voluminous busted Sissy Lady here in the front row. Next to the Sissy-Gurl I insulted.

Thank you Professor, I'm Mary. By your description Professor it does sound like a really interesting and juicy orgasmic topic, but I'm also a little confused and frightened as well. So who does the Homo-Femininus have sex with again?

Glad you asked Mary, Homo-Femininus® Sissies, only have sex with Sissies. And you're Mary Dune aren't you?

Yes, (Mary answers with a bewildered look on her face) Professor, I'm Mary Dune.

Oh! I watched a video up on the internet before class about you. It went viral with sixty-nine million views on **SissyTube**®, very impressive!

What? (Mary is stunned and covers her face. She can't believe what she was told). Of me Professor?

Yes Mary, you're somewhat of celebrity now. The video was taken of you speaking in Professor Yaoi's Sissyology class this morning.

Oh I didn't know about the video Professor.

Yeah the video is huge! And it's good to see FUCIT students are being recognized on a global scale for their stand on issues in the Sissydom® community. Bravo to both of you, good job!

Thanks Professor. And my colleague Professor Yaoi gave me a heads up about the two of you.

What? Oh my Cock-God! (Jane also covers her face with her hands in disbelief).

So, Good job you two! You should be very proud of your Sissy selves. Way-to-go!

[2.5] FEMCOCK

Professor!

Yes. The big fellow way up in the back, what's your question?

So, can a **Stud**® screw a Homo-Femininus Sissy in the ass, like we do the predominant, faggot type Sissy?

Oh! Again sorry about the confusion! The Homo-Femininus® type Sissy does NOT take Studs up the Vaganus® like the regular Sissies do. So, for clarity, the Homo-Femininus is the, Fucker not the Fuckee.

And my friend, no offense intended but, stop calling **Sissy-Gurls**®, faggots. It's not only an incorrect categorization of an entire Sub-Class of society in the MSES, but also offensive too many in the Sissydom® community. Not to mention, you can be castrated for breaking the law against **Profanity** [17.34]. Use of a disrespectful accusation regarding sexual orientation is forbidden! I noticed you **Stud**® folks love calling Sissies faggot, gay, queer, femboy, shemale, trannys, homo, all of which are references to Homo-Sapiens not Homo-Sis-Sapiens. So just a word to the wise. I will dock you points for incorrect genome referencing on your papers. You can reference the **Genomes** [18] of the MSES in manual SM069.

Okay, but let's get back to Mary's question. Who do Homo-Femininus® have sex with? Well, first let me stop here to re-word the medical term for Homo-Femininus as its street name, FEMCOCK or for short just FEM®. These FEMs would obviously need to penetrate a sex partner to gain pleasure considering their immense penis size. We all know the **Sex-Laws**© [7], but biologically who do you think they would prefer to perform coitus with a Girl or a Boy? So can anyone tell which of the two of these genders is preferred by the FEM? Yes, the buff Sissy-Trainer looking young man with the huge biceps.

Well Professor you said the FEM was both gay and a Sissy so I'm figuring, the FEM likes to have sex with men and or women, just like a Sissy who swings both ways.

Yes, young man you're right to a certain degree.

FEMs would have sex with men or women as any Sissy would. But remember this from the Sex-Laws, homosexuality and gayness is illegal in the USA Inc. And is so by the partial ratification of the twenty-ninth **Amendment** [17.29.1]. And later set into law by a Presidential Executive Order. These laws set the new morality rules for our Nation which makes it legal for men to perform compensation and recreational sex with Sissies. And, wait. Because this is the part which will astonish you!

Because the Sissy type of FEMCOCK® has been gender designated a male by the Bureau of Sex Classification, the **BSC**

[4.D-G6.4] and a Sissy by the Department of Health and Mind Control, the FEM may engage in sex with ONLY a Sissy® or a **Sissy-Breeder**® woman. But they may NEVER engage in sex with men as regular normal Sissies do. Remember, Sissies can engage in sex with men because they are classified by the Bureau of Sex Classification as being female despite the fact that they do NOT have a fully functional non-dormant baby-making uterus! Go figure!

Professor, do you mean the Sissy Gurls can't give birth?

No they cannot! But like I said, there are gene scientists working on a fix. Oh and by the way, the dormant inactive uterus is an effect of gene modification. I mean, if the United States Inc. government wanted Sissies to get pregnant with monkey babies they would have given them one that works.

Mary what the hell is she talking about? (Jane is seriously questioning if this Professor is firing on all her cylinders).

Class, let me set you straight here! I've studied Sissyology all of my life. Heck! I have a doctorate degree in the dam subject, and I always get confused explaining the **FEM**®. So, don't feel bad about your confusion. If you remember anything we studied today or this semester remember this one thing, FEMs are a sub-class of the **Whore**® class and is the only male group in the Sissy social class of the MSES®. Word to the wise-student, get this right on the final exam and you pretty much pass the course. Haaa... haa... Just kidding, not.

Okay! Also don't forget this important fact. The **Sissy**® culture is the only official social class in the United States which can legally participate in providing recreational and monetary transactions for labor compensation. This process is also known as **LCT**® [4.D-G2.27]. These transactions are available only to the working male population in the USA Inc. in the Modern Socio-Economic System. And this has everything to do with what I mentioned earlier about the, MSES compensation system.

So, after all of that lengthy explanation, is there a choice of who a FEM may legally have sex with? I'll spare you the embarrassment, the answer is NO! And because of the discombobulated bi-partisan oversight nature of our Cunt-gress in Washingcum they can only have coitus with a SISSY!

Professor! How are they bred? I mean, where do they cum from?

Good question! As far as breeding. With Sissy-Breeder mommies of course. Although there are members of the US Cunt-gress who are trying to pass a bill banning FEM breeding. But I'm not sure what's going to happen. Regardless if a law passes, currently FEMs happen to be born out of sheer coincidence. FEMs have only been bred from Sissy-Parents. And FEMs have the same civil rights, benefits and privileges, defined in the thirtieth Amendment [17.30] as do the, normal, everyday, Sissy-Gurls who you Studs so often and wantonly screw.

[2.6] POTION

Rimme has a private conversation with Mary...

So let's take a short ten minute break so all of this can soak in. Miss Dune, could I please have a private word with you please? (Rimme motions with her hand for Mary to cum closer).

Ahhh... What do you think she wants Mary? I don't know Jane, let go of my hand Darling. Wait outside in the hallway I gotta go talk to her. Mwah...

Yes, Professor Rimme!

Mwah… Yeah, I'll wait right outside the lecture hall Mary. Okay Babe. Kiss.

Yeah, yeah… And try not to get into trouble Jane. Kiss....

Miss Dune, (Rimme extends her hand to shake Mary's but afterwards doesn't let go of it). As the Head of the Sissyology Department, I'll also be at the **NSA** [4.D-G6.13] meeting on Friday with Professor Yaoi.

Great Professor! Glad to hear it! (Mary realizes, Rimme is twice her size and the Professors grip on her hand is so strong it would be futile to break). I've read all of your books and published academic journal papers Professor and it's an honor to be in your class.

Well, thank you Mary. I've also browsed your academic file and was very impressed.

Professor, Jane and I.

Oh Mary! I do hope Miss Goldberg accepted my apology in class today.

Ah Professor! Don't worry about Jane. She's just a live wire, always standing up for Sissy rights. Ummm… (Mary is getting a little dizzy).

Yes Mary, Jane definitely has Sissy Pride this is for sure.

Yeah! That's my Gurl. Jane and I are Sissy-Promised® to each other and we're planning on getting married.

Oh! Well, congratulations. DOM-Bitch marriages are rare.

Thanks Professor. I was going to tell you we're both excited about the possible **NSA** [4.D-G6.13] opportunity you're offering us. And Thank you for selecting Jane and I we look forward to participating in the NSA program. Ummm... (Mary feels faint).

Oh! Well Thank you my dear (Professor Rimme is holding Mary's hand rubbing a sticky sperm smelling gel into her palm) it's a pleasure (Mary smells the cummy smell from the gel but her mind starts to drift off) to have students who (Mary is starting to feel like she's gonna faint) enjoy participating intimately.

Hmmm... Oooh, Professor? Oooh! Uuuum... I... I, I think! Aaaah Prof Rim... Meee.

Mary here, please sit down my dear you look dizzy. You will make a promise to me Mary. (Mary's head is spinning, the Love-Potion® Rimme has been rubbing into her palm has Mary in a trance).

Yes Professor. Rim...Mee. And make a promise.

Yes, you are promised to Jane. You will also promise yourself to me Mary. I will own you Mary.

Yes, Prof Rim Me. Own me!

That's right Mary I will rim you for your own good, I will rim you frequently, many, many times. Now go back to Jane and hold her hand because you're Promised to Jane and you'll also be promised to me as well.

Yes, Professor Rim Me.

Mary who are you promised to?

I'm promised to you and Jane, Prof Rim Me.

This is right Mary! Now go back to Jane your lover and lifelong companion. (Rimme helps her from the seat and directs her on the way back towards Jane who is already back from break).

Several minutes later...

Mwah... What did she say? (Jane asks as they sit back in their seats).

What? (Mary has a zombie stare in her eyes and mumbles her response).

What did Professor Rimme say to you? (Jane is in anticipation of some juicy news).

Say? Say what? (Spaced out Mary is incoherent).

Huh! Mary! Hello! (Jane waves her hand in front of Mary's eyes). Mare, what did she say?

Ahhhh... Aaaah. I don't remember!

Huh! What do you mean you don't remember it was a minute ago? Are you on drugs? Mary? Wait! Did you guys just have sex? Is this an orgasmic high?

Yeah, hey Jane. Mwah... I'm Sissy-Promised to you Jane.

Ahhh... Yeah I know. What's happening? We're in Sex Psychology class. (Jane shakes Mary by the shoulders to revive her) Mary wake up Sissy-Gurl? (Jane taps Mary on her cheek lightly). Sap out of it!

[2.7] BREAKS OVER

Welcome back to class, is everybody here? (Rimme looks over to checks if Mary is cognizant enough). Okay, somewhat here at least I think.

I think everybody is back, Professor.

Okay! So now that we have defined who the FEM can have sex with, Sissies only. Let's analyze the psychological, sexual and physical relationship between the **Sissy-Gurl**® and the **FEM**®.

To analysis the pair more closely, let's look at both. The majority, the prevalent Sissy is the feminine little Cocklet or Clit, either **DOM**® or **Bitch**® respectively. These Gurls put out Vaganus® to anyone who has performed labor. And this is providing there are enough Male-Orgasms, **MO**® [12.L1.1] credits in the system needed to be compensated to them for work they've preformed.

And the second type of Sissy is the smallest minority in Sissydom and is sexually active in different ways. The **FEM**® type of Sissy does NOT provide hole to the sexual partner as the normal Sissy does. Instead they insert their long appendages into Sissy-Gurls.

Huh! Okay, I know what you're thinking, so what! Everybody screws Sissies. Well here's the amazing part, with no help from other men, the FEM® type can easily fuck-out, **FO**® [16.7] a Sissy-Gurl using only their monstrous sized male appendage. And stop and fathom this thought for a moment here! Considering it takes a minimum of over six hundred and ninety pricks to **FO**® the average mutated humanoid purebred Sissy. Yet the FEM accomplishes this solely by using his-her enormous dick alone! And often times with just several thrusts! Now that's amazing! And bear in mind the FEMs all have dicks longer and thicker than any human Stud® penis. With the longest recorded FEM penis size being sixteen point nine inches long and three inches wide. A truly Massive COCK!

Huh! Ooooh! Ahhh... (Some of the Sissy Gurls student feel faint just thinking of its massiveness).

Colossal... !!!...

Haa haaa... Despite the enormity of their penis, appearance-wise it is difficult to recognize a **FEM®**. Mainly because, they dress pretty-much like your average Stud® Lady. Very conservatively by modern standards. With skirts or dresses with a minimum of just below the knee length. For example, like the dress I have on today would be what a FEM Sissy wears. And they also have very large breasts, coincidentally very similar to my own bust. We won't even consider Non-Stud working class woman here, Modern-Scank is not the style FEMs are into.

And unlike their **Sissy®** counterparts, like for example Miss Goldberg here, with her exposed, well, everything! FEM Ladies never expose their private parts. In fact there has never been a photograph or video taken of them. Except of course for the ones confiscated and or destroyed by the **DHMC®** [4.D-G6.1]. They have never displayed their massive male appendages in public. And like Stud Ladies they have never expose their beasts or have gone bare-chested in public, again, for example never like Miss Goldberg's hard aroused nipples revealed by her cup-less bra.

Oh! Miss **Goldberg**, you don't mind if I use you as an example for the class, do you?

No, Professor please use me I'm a Sissy. (Jane stands up turns to her classmates and throws out her chest proudly, while tweaking both her nipples)

Whoohooo! Hoe Bag! Yeah! Hoo! Slut! You Whore! Whohooo! Show us everything bitch! You Hoe! (The Stud students express their desires).

Thank you for this unneeded display Miss Goldberg. Okay, settle down, that's enough. Miss Goldberg I'd like to remind you about the illicit titillation rule, **SITR**® [15-69.0]. Performed lewd acts by a Sissy is illegal.

Sorry Professor. (Jane bashfully hangs her head and says).

Now back to… Oh yeah! The simplest way to understand the difference is, one type of Sissy bends over for the FEM Sissy to bang them in their **Vaganus**®. The other type of Sissy, the one who is literally hung like a horse, bends the Sissy-Gurl over and rims out the little feminine **Gurl**®. But you college kids are smart enough to know this.

[2.8] WHY

Global dominance using pure American Vaganus…

And here's a point you freshmen have to be clear on if you're going to study Sissydom here in the United States Inc. Basically in the case of the Sissies it's a legal issue as far as who gets it up the ass. Huh! I'm sorry! In the Vaganus®. This is because by law like I've said, men CANNOT do men in the ass anymore. In other words, having conventional Man-on-Man, **MOM**® sex is called Gay and it is illegal now in the year 2251. The United States is way to morally correct with the adoption of Sissydom to condone Gay-Sex.

But, even though illegal, Gay citizens are part of the Whoring Industry. Most registered Gay members of society are professional Sissy-in-Training, **SIT**® [1.A2.4] instructors. They are all an integral part of the Sissification process.

Ahhhh…. Where were we? (Rimme twirls her hair).

Gayness Professor! (Mary shouts).

Yeah, yeah… Ah and here's where most folks lose the true meaning of **Sissydom**® and its integration into American life. I'll clarify something here, and this is important. Class in our Cunt-trie, gay-sex has be cum illegal not because of moral issues, quite the contrary. In fact to prove my point, even the old dysfunctional monetary system, the fractional reserve banking system in this Cunt-trie was designed by private bankers in a structure to inflict as much anal pressure on its depositors and debtors as possible. So financially speaking, Americans have always had something up their ass, gay or not! We always have private debt to the banks and tax debt to the government.

It's this mix of money, sex and government which makes the USA Inc. poised to be the next worlds Super-Power through its total control of Sissydom. And globally speaking, the United States does have the ultimate solution by aspiring to globally have an American Vaganus in every home in the world. And of course, Americans would conveniently profit financially from every penetration and subsequent ad-Dick-tion to Vaganus. This would truly return global domination back to the United States.

At this point and I'm off topic, you might be, and I certainly hope you are, wondering who the culprits were in the pre-second US Cunt-stitution economy that destroyed the most prosperous nation on Earth? Well it was the Federal Reserve Bank, the **FED**® [23.11] for short. It was metaphorically speaking openly, screwing our government and the US population in the ass when they were printing all of the trillions of fiat US dollars. Then the FED used the funny money to buy US Treasury bonds, aka Ponzi scheme. Ahhh, I digress...

Aaah... Where were we? Oh yeah! Back to anal-sex. Gay sex, has been renamed to Man-on-Man, MOM® and is illegal in most circumstances. Because after the financial crises of 2007 the disillusioned American males changed their sexual orientation from a vagina to ass-pussy. And back in the day, before the creation of the Homo-Sis-Sapien genome, an ass-pussy was actually referred to as an, *asshole* by some most folks. But besides what you wanna call a screw-hole, my main point here is this, after the financial crisis of 2007, the American male could not afford to raise a family in the United States. Men, by no fault of their own, changed their sexual orientation.

Talk about screwing people in the ass! Here's a historical side note. The USA Inc. had a long history, of about a hundred or more years of screwing people and taking their natural resources, also known as, interventionism. Which is a form of political sodomy disguised as democracy?

Professor! (Mary calls out).

Yes, the astute Mary Dune?

Professor would you suggest reading the Rise and Fall of the American Penis to those wishing to know more about the demise of America in that era?

Absolutely! Without a doubt the most definitive novels of that period. An epic literary work by Seymour Goldberg.

Thank you Professor. (Mary says and winks at Rimme).

Huh! Ha haaa... (Rimme smiles and winks back at Mary). Right now you're all probably scratching your heads wondering how a once great nation like the United States could have ever be cum so screwed up. I mean it's the only Cunt-tree in the world which replaced vaginal intercourse with Vaganus® regulated Sissy-Sex. I mean, how screwed up is that? Well, there're a lot of psychological theories out there about this American phenomena. All the research tries to justify screwing people in the ass as a solution to monetary problems.

But after decades of analysis, the general consensus is, the sexual change of which hole to screw stems from a Monkey-see-Monkey-do scenario. Where our government was seen as the Fucker and the US citizens assume the bitch position as the Fuckee. Then of course the US citizens just started mounting anything in sight, aka ass-pussy.

Besides sodomy was the hard working American males expression of its true hatred it felt towards the United States government due to its governments destruction of a once prosperous working class from which the working American male had belonged prior to outsourcing.

So some of you might be saying, Professor why break-up the party, why make gayness illegal if Americans prefer to do people in the ass, why not leave well enough alone? Well yes they would have but, there was an obvious shortage problem, supply-and-demand economics. The amount of gay men willing to prostitute themselves out was very limited and the United States government had to step in and take charge of the situation by implementing the **MSES®**. It was an intervention.

You see, this is the American-way of conflict resolution. For example after the 2007 financial crisis our government here in the US produced fiat money as a financial stimulus for its corporate masters and banking buddies on Wall-Street. And nowadays it produces ass-pussy also known as Sissies as a monetary stimulus.

In fact there're even new economic theories based on the relationship between economic systems and Sissydom®. At **Hardon-Vard** University and also here at FUCIT there are new courses offered in, Financial Vaganus **Economics** [21.B.15]. This new Vaganus economics theory has Ponzi scheme written all over it, as does every financial theory. But the Financial Vaganus theory is being embraced now because it has less joblessness and starvation associated with it, than the old Keynesian economics did.

And there you have it boys, girls and Gurls, why 6.9 percent of the American population is being breed into existence to be Sissy Whores®.

[2.9] FEM RESEARCH

Now knowing what we just went over, you can understand why the FEMs are seen in the likeness of our previous government here in the United States. Both are the perpetrators, and the Sissy, the one's being physically sodomized, who depicts the American working class taking financially-sodomy. So remember, even though they are Sissies, the FEMs are seen to have the upper hand and a very similar resemblance to our government officials. And a perfect likeness to our government's crony private banking buddies. The FEMs usually go an entire lifetime without taking a single physical or financial debt creating dick up their wealthy asses. Truly amazing! Zero liability, simply shocking!

For that matter, according to the new Financial Anal Economic theory, American businesses, bankers, FEMs and the USA Inc.

government, has or assumes none of the, debt, blame, or responsibility for the misery it has inflicted on the world's populations through Vaganus® ad-Dick-tion.

So in conclusion, and I'm sure you're bored with this stuff by now, it leaves only the predominant tiny-cockette vulnerable type of Sissy to service the FEMs gargantuan penises. Scary! I know, but this is the same type of situation our Stud® class males are masters at. They have a primitive need to screw the Sissy® when they are not or are married to a Stud-Breeder® lady.

Albeit, a FEM doing a Sissy in the Vaganus® is still rare due to the fact that there's estimated only to be approximately six hundred ninety FEM type Sissies in existence in the USA. And the FEM as well as normal Sissies are band in every Cunt-tree in the world except the USA Inc. But regardless of the infrequency of the sex, there have been some studies which describe the sex between these two types of Sissies as memorable, to say the least. So any questions?

Yes, over here, the Stud breeding young Lady.

Professor what do you mean it's memorable?

Oh well in my new book,

Sissyology
where are we going and will we ever get there?

I devoted an entire chapter to FEMs and their unusual, uncanny ability to totally control a Sissy Gurl® with nothing more than their magnificent male appendage.

It's been documented, by researchers here at the FUCIT Institute of Sexual Arousal, when a FEM rims a Sissy Gurl® it is an unforgettable event who the tiny peanut-size clit Sissy never forgets in their entire lifetimes. This by the way only serves to create feelings of dependence on the FEMs. Because after sex with a FEM the Sissy realizes they just had the most mind blowing sex of their lives and sex without a FEM would be trivial in comparison.

Though there are side effects experienced by the Sissies who are preyed upon by the FEMs. For example, there are recorded cases of Sissies being hospitalized after a FEM has mounted the lovehole of the privileged Sissy. And typically the Sissy-Gurl must refrain from engaging in sex for several days or longer after being rimmed by a FEM. Not only because they're so sore they can't walk straight but also because of the pints of FEM-Cream® which has been implanted into the Sissies puss. The cream, is not only an aphrodisiac but also a mind controlling and numbing hallucinogenic as well, which by the way, is found nowhere else in nature except in FEM sperm.

[2.10] PHENOMENA

On a sociological note. How did all this cum to be? As I've stated, there's a correlation between the FEMs and our previous American government here in the United States. And from inconclusive anthro-sis-pology studies conducted, we can assume the myths handed down claiming the FEM has been around for centuries are true. Although none of these claims have been confirmed, substantiated or proven and are assumed, by some, to be nothing more than folk tales. The realistic explanation according to the USA Inc. is, through the miracle of modern American Sissy-Science, the **Sissification**® drugs have produced the irregular phenomena. But this was not the original intention of our bio-genetic engineers who invented the

Sissification drugs. They didn't want to produce a Sissy creature with an extremely long penis, which have an insatiable desire to screw young innocent Gurls!

And the aphrodisiac, mind controlling, hallucinogenic effect of the FEM cream is also an abnormality. But FEMs are considered a well cumed mutation none the less. Because being dosed by their special type of Man-Cream is not known to have any detrimental effects socially, physically or mentally.

Also class, I mentioned the large voluminous amount of **FEM-Cream**® produced by these freaks. This is designed into the normal Sissy-Gurl genetics, to produce larger volumes of Jizzies. However this was only because the scientists knew the Sissy-**Gurl**® would be engaged sexually with many sex partners and process **LCT**® constantly. So to emulate the Sissies continued participation in the sex-act, also to enhance the sexual experience of the male participant, they genetically designed the Sissies clits to squirt copious amounts of Jizzies. This just carried over into the FEMs physiology but to an extreme degree. The FEMs huge nut-sack produces several pints of intoxicating cream per dosing and quarts per day. They are total amazing virile creatures!

[2.11] PAIRS

Pimp-Whore, Master-Slave analogy...

Again, to make this topic more palatable, I'll use the analogy of pimp-whore and its resemblance to the government-citizen pair. Now sociologically the scientists definitely did not want to produce a Predator-Prey social imbalance as did the Federal Reserve Bank. In fact the relationship between the FEM-Sissy-Gurl pair has been determined by the US Department of Commerce to be more of a **Pimp-Whore**® business relationship. Where the Pimp is the FEM as were the Wall Street bankers and for profit they controlled is the sexual activity of the common Sissy-Gurl Whore®. And in this case the Whore® represents the vulnerable US citizen. How the biological instincts of both types play out in the Pimp-Whore relationship is as follows and you can find this in the Sissy Manual as well See: SM069, Section 8 Appendix H, **Pimp-Whore®** [8.1]. Here I'll continue with the analogy,

(1) The FEM® plays the dominant role in the relationship (government).

(2) The Sissy® gladly assumes the submissive feminine role (citizen).

Putting it differently, by naturally occurring events, the FEM selects a pure Breed-from-Birth, **BfB®** Sissy to be cum his-her bitch and this is regardless of the Sissy being in either a Sissy-Promise and or a Sissy-Breeding Marriage with a Sissy-Breeding human female wife and or Sissy-Married to another Sissy.

So! To amalgamate the pair the FEM coerces the naive Sissy to undergo the following steps to be ritualistically made into the Pimps Bitch **(1) Selected (2) Dosed (3) Declared (4) Branded.**

The chosen Sissies usually live normal lives regardless of being inoculated (dosed) with the controlling substance of the FEMs love cream or not. And in no way does the Pimp disturb the emotional balance of society by altering previous marital and or social obligations made by the pimps prey. In a minute, I'll go over some of the official ethics, rules and restrictions placed on this complex Whore-Pimp® relationship between a FEM and a Gurl.

Like I said, nature takes over, so let's quickly go over the biological and ritualistic process of forming the relationship one step at a time. This process is sometimes referred to by its scientific name, Bitchification®. Again refer to the SM069 for all the details [8.H1].

(H1) **Pimp-Whore**® Inoculation Procedure or Bitchification

But here I'll give you the short version.

(1) Selection: the FEMCOCK chooses his vulnerable prey.

(2) Dosing: Sissy is inoculated with Pimps FEM-Cream®.

(3) Declaration: Pimp proclaims ownership of the chosen Sissy.

(4) Branding: Pimped Whore is branded with the symbol of the Pimp Whore Partnership (PWP). The Pimp uses a flesh burning hot branding iron to declare the newly consummated Whore to be his Bitch.

Ahhh! That's Gruesome Professor! Uooogh! It's horrible! (The Sissy students grumble about the inhumane techniques).

Yes, yes… Well the Sissy is sedated at the time and feels absolutely no pain during the entire Bitchification. So don't get your pretty little panties in a wad about it! Besides, the Sissy® is just a live-stock animal used for sex. And on the few remaining animal ranches still in existence in America the animals are still branded for identification, as is every citizen with an RFID chip.

But some of the after-effects of being made into a branded Pimped-Whore® and Bitch are as follows. Nobody who is penetrated by a FEM® ever forgets the sensation of the over-powering effect of their predators inoculation. Once the FEM has ejaculated Pimp-Cream into the Sissy, the Sissy feels like she has been spiritually transformed by the Pimp. The Sissies mind starts to experience hallucinations and goes into a semi-conscience trance state. This is when the hardly understood event happens, where the Sissy is mind altered into be cuming a slave of their Pimp. And will not obey the command of other Pimps. They are subservient to only one Pimp at a time and in the frail mind of the inoculated Sissy the Pimp is the Sissies god-like Master to be praised and worshiped forever.

Wow! Oooh! Professor how is this possible? (All the Sissy Gurls are startled by the lecture and squirm in their seats while ejaculating Jizzies into their socks).

Gurls! Gurls! Please calm down! Okay, are there any questions?

Yes, the DOM Lady being swarmed over by Studs. Boys! Please sit down, thank you!

Professor! Should I be worried about being inoculated by a FEM Pimp and does the Pimps Love Juice wear off if the Sissy douches-out her pussy?

Excellent questions! No, there has never been a fatality or injury caused by being made into a Pimps Whore or Bitch. Also there has never been a Sissy abuse complaint filed with the Department of Health and Mind Control, the DHMC. And bare-in-mind, in America only FEMs can be registered Pimps. So, this thing about Pimps is a very guarded and well controlled part of the whole system of worker compensation in the MSES. We'll get to the PWP rules and regulations in a moment.

[2.12] PWP

Being in a Pimp/Whore partnership or a **PWP**® [8.H2] as it's called, with a FEM has been described by actual Sissy testimony as, paradise, a type of Shangri-La. This unusual relationship is considered by many in academia and by Sissy scholars as well as Sissyologists to be the epitome of what Sissydom® is all about. The PWP® is considered very beneficial to all parties involved. There're even Sissies who have stalked FEMs for the chance to be made into one of their harem Whores. So to a Common Sissy, or what's referred to as an un-pimped Sissy, it's considered to be a privilege and an honor to be made into a Pimped-Whore® and branded as a Pimps Bitch.

Oooh! Wow! Amazing! I would love to be Pimped! (The Sissy Gurls are all a glee about with prospects of being corralled into a harem).

I take it by some of your expressions and the looks on your faces that I've sparked an interest with the introduction of the FEM mutation. Hmmm… But for you vulnerable young naïve Gurls a word of caution is necessary. So, I apologize for making sex-slavery sound like an effortless free-lunch. Believe me, domination is no picnic.

I'll redefine it here. As far as the domination of the Pimp-Master of the Whore-Slave, think of it this way, the Sissy is typically cum-manded by their Master to perform sex. Usually very pleasurable sex I might add. And I repeat there has never been a complaint filed against FEMs for Sissy abuse. Quite the contrary, there are well known Sissy authors who have written many books on the subject of the Pimp Whore Partnerships and Pimp Harems (PWH). All of which have praised the cultural significance of having PWPs and PWHs in the twenty-third century.

And no to your second question, the magic Pimp-Cream® of the FEM gives the Sissy the feeling of being totally controlled by her Pimp is merely a psychological side effect and is more of a spiritual condition of the **Sex-Soul** [21.B.24.2].

Mind you, it's a condition because, while yes, the Sissy is in a mind-numbing trance, more than that, she's transformed into a zombie obeying her Masters every cum-mand. More or less as the American tax payers were prior to the US dollar collapse.

And No! You Sissies are not going to get pregnant! I get asked this all the time. So, anyway, the answer is, no, the Masters inoculation wears off after six point nine weeks. But when the Sissy is dosed their pussy belongs to their Master or Pimp whatever you want to call them. Not just because of the neurochemical effect on the Gurls body by the special love potion cream but also because, and we already went over this, the Sissy knows there is no replacement for the sexual satisfaction the FEM gave her.

And this is why Pimps will bang all the Whores in their harem at least once every six point nine days. Not just to dose them with their love-potion but also to develop the physical bond between the Pimp and soon to be ad-Dick-ted Whore. This physical dependency on their Pimps penis, most always, turns the Pimp-Whore relationship into a lifelong one. The longing for their Master keeps them wanting to remain members of their Pimps Harem.

Let me remind you here because we're talking about the chronological aspect of the PWP. FEMs only have sex six to nine times a day in a very ritualistic fashion. Yeah surprise! Pimps don't do quickies with their Whores. So, doing the math, the FEM Pimp cannot mathematically have an unlimited amount of Sissies under his-her control at any one time in his-her harem. Notice I'm speaking of Whores in the plural. Questions?

Yes, the Stud drooling on the attractive DOM.

So Professor can Pimps practice polygamy?

Yes they can! But not in the sense the Whores in their harem are his wives. Not at all like Stud® husbands here in the United States do since polygamy was legalized. For details refer to **Amendment** 29, [17.29.2].

So no, the FEM® doesn't practice polygamy like most American's. The harem is more of a sexual spiritualism, religious-for-profit endeavor than a marriage. And although there are documented cases of Sissies falling in love with their Pimp, most of the Whore-Pimp relationships are based on the Whore worshipping the shear magnificence, size and sexual power of the FEMs penis and not the Pimp herself.

As I was saying, regardless of the overwhelming amount of young Sissy Whores willing to sacrifice themselves to FEMs just for the opportunity to worship the Pimps. The FEMs are strictly regulated by the US Federal Government as are all facets of the MSES®. FEMs and Sissies are the only groups of MSES who can be involved in a Pimp Whore Partnerships. And again I'm always amazed by the startling similarity between the Pimp-Sissy relationship and the Wall-Street Banker and the money-whoring politicians of the previous fascist US government.

[2.13] RULES

Like I said, we are going to go over briefly the rules governing the facilitation of Sissy Cunts. For the full definition refer to the following, Partnership [8], Appendix H, Part A (1-7) and Part B (8-14).

So here's the short version, According to the Pimp Whore Partnership (PWP) rules and regulations set by Cunt-gress and the US Department of Commerce, Sissy Trade Division (STD), to control the procurement and subsequent usury of the Sissy Whore.

(1) The Pimp can only have six haremized Sissy slaves.

(2) The Sissy must follow the Sissy Code of Whoring Ethics.

(3) The Whore rules apply to Whores under the influence.

(4) The Whore may request termination of services.

(5) The Whore is always compensated for her services.

(6) The Whore may be pimped-out by the Pimp to Studs.

(7) Only a FEMCOCK can be registered as a Pimp.

(8) The Pimp can only have one Harem.

(9) The Whore must be approved by a committee of Pimps.

(10) Whores may do a, **Choosey Susie** to change Pimps.

(11) Whores may be a member of only one Harem.

(12) The Whore may only be branded once.

(13) Pimps can never be married to a Whore.

One specific PWP rule stands out to me. The note reads as follows. And I will not repeat this! Rule number (6). These Stud Class members mentioned usually have a SCR of L12 or higher and never commence coitus with Common C-type Hoe Sissies.

[2.14] HAREM CULTURE

Okay! This is the last section for today. Culturally speaking though, like I've said there is usually a very strong bond developed between the branded Sissy Whores and the Pimp who owns her. It's something about serving her Master which makes the relationships very meaningful. In fact although only one Whore is dosed at a time, the other Harem Whores usually participate in the ritual. They often times do fluffing or performing cleaning of excess Love-Potion® from the Sissies over-flowing Vaganus®. And or lapping up sweet tasting Sissy-Poop® after the inoculation process. Haremized Sissy Whores occasionally fall in love with each other and or form lifelong emotional relationships.

The relationships Whores forge with their Pimp has been known to last even after the Sissy has left the Harem and is no longer being controlled by her Masters Pimp-Cream. And this is also regardless of whether the Whore is an active harem member or has relocated for academic or career reasons far from their Pimps harem.

Pimped Whores when and if they are freed, are usually promoted by their Pimp to a higher position called a Free Pimped-Whore or a **FPW**® [8.H3.14] which are classified as Non-Harem Bitches of the Pimp and typically remain servants on contract to their Pimp for life. Also the FPWs are permanent members of the United States Sissy Reserves, **USSR**® [25.26.2] until retirement age. Harem-Bitches in the Reserves may be called up for active duty at any time. For example, in the case of a National sexual emergency, like a shortage of Pimped-Whores to run for a Cunt-gressional seat or some other sexual economic catastrophe.

Ahhh…. This is a typical question. Rule number (12) about the branding. Usually the Sissies are branded on their left ass cheeks with the PWP symbol which also has below the symbol the Whores serial number issued by the Pimp the Whore belongs too. The significance of branding of the Whore® is a way of permanently marking her as having been made into the property of their Pimp. Much the way livestock is branded. But it's more for display in modern times here in the USA Inc. because like I said, every US citizen has had an RFID chip implanted in them. So in reality all US citizens, Sissies or not, are basically like live-stock animals.

And to expand on this. For Sissies the brand on their ass is often displayed in public as a badge of honor to indicate they were chosen and have the privilege to be a Pimped-Whore® and not just a common C-Type Hoe. In Sissydom® a branded Sissy has rank and authority over all other Sissies and because they are branded they have special privileges outside of the Sissy Cum-munity as well. This includes running for public office, promotions in the military, banking, tenure at a university, etc.

But! As glamorous as all this may sound, due to the FEMs very selective inoculation process, very few Sissies have the pleasure of receiving the FEMs magic-love probe up their Sissy cooch.

Professor what's a Cooch?

Oh please! Look it up at, Urban Dictionary dot com.

Huh! Okay the very, very last point. If you've studied the history of Sissyology you'd know about a culture of men known as Shemales or Transgender. They were persecuted by the US government for centuries and hunted down as domestic terrorists. Oddly enough, the FEM® mutation is very closely related to the social phenomena called, Shemales, but not genetically in anyway. If you're not familiar with this part of ancient human LGBT history I suggest reading a book entitled, *Do Me I'm a Dickgirl* by a very famous Sissy author called Fuckuous.

Now, this is not a Second US **Cunt-stitution** [17] History class. It's a Sex Psychology course so to stay on topic. Let's explore the chart on page 69 of the thought patterns of the mutated humanoid mind of the FEMs. And notice the similarity to the once thought to be, normal human brain patterns of the money-whoring narcissistic and greed infected corrupt mind of the Neo-Fascists from the old United States government, prior to the partial ratification of the **Cunt-stitution**. These criminals were....

Professor we're out of time. (Jane shouts).

Oh, Okay thank you Miss Goldberg. This was too much for one day anyway. Well, I want you all to go online and check the class assignment I posted. Read Chapter 6 section 9 in your textbooks, on the Behavioral Engineering of Americans. And see yah on Thursday now,

GET OUT OF HERE...!!!.... (Rimme shouts).

[2.15] AFTER CLASS

Holy-Cock! That's was a really, really long lecture.

Yep! Mwah... But we made it! We survived our first day of college, Wooohooo..!!!...

Hey let's hit a Whoring-Station (WS) on campus on the way back to the dorm for some celebration sex and dinner.

Celebration for sure Lover! Mwah... Besides I'm starving for some dick milk after all that talk about FEMs and their massive male organs. Huh! My heads swimming!

Mwah... Yeah, me too, I kept having orgasms through the whole lecture. And I can really use a good rimming. (Mary plays with her erect three inch Gurl-Clit) Maybe after our WS® obligation we can get a **Studbucks**® hot latte Man-Cream.

Yeah, yeah… Mary, it's cool they have a **Studbucks**® in all the Whoring Stations and hey, the Sissy frapa-poop-uccino drink is the bomb! Hmm... Hmmm… Tasty!

The Gurls skip away hand-in-hand to the WS…

Hey, did you notice anything unusual about Professors Yaoi or Rimme?

Ummm… I don't know! Other than getting really dizzy when and after I spoke with her and couldn't remember a dam thing she said to me. Ahhhh… They're beautiful, tall, shapely women. All I know is they dress like old Stud-Ladies. No, actually more like old grandmothers.

Yeah but they were too young to be dressed like that.

True, you got that right Mare. But hey! I think a skirtini is long. Still there was something about them both I found attractive. I mean their hair, nails, make-up were impeccable. Really refined, sophisticated, beautiful, classy ladies for sure and those huge tits! I was salivating.

Oooh yeah! They looked hot like your tits Babe. Mwah…

Mwah… Oooh! Cum here Honey-Bunny. Hmmm... Kisss... I love you Jane.

Yeah! And everything about them. Their walk and talk was intoxicating. I don't know Honey. Mwah… It doesn't explain the stuffy old conservative long dress style. I know it's not the instructor's dress code, because I've seen instructors walking around in mini-skirt and transparent blouses.

Yeah! Maybe they're just weird?

Mwah… I don't care Jane! I would eat-out both of their cunts for an **NSA** scholarship.

[2.16] WS6969C

Dinnertime at the Whoring Station…

Here we are, Whoring-Station 6969C.

Perfect I'm going to down a gallon of Man-Cream®.

Mwah… Sounds good to me Sweetheart! I wanna take it up my cunts too, I'm kind of dry (Jane fingers her Sissy-Puss).

Hey! Don't forget, we only have a couple of hours to play.

Yeah sure, but we have to perform a minimum of 6 to 9 penetrations for Cum-munity service at a public C-Type Whoring-Station® per day. I never understood the classification bullshit of Whoring-Stations, **WH®** [7.G4]. Common (C), Student (S), Restricted (R), Limited (L). I mean, Geeeez! It's a place to go and mount a Sissy in the ass-cunt. Why make it more complicated than that?

Well my rule hating friend, C because some men are particular where they stick their dicks and at a Common WS, they only have access to registered whores who are, **PSW®** or lower, like our dads. And if the Sissy is PSW or less she's usually called a Hoe. If the WH is an **RS** type, like the one at our dorm, the Sissy

Whores are students and we have the rights to be able to studying while fulfilling our **WH**® duties.

Right, right… And the Restricted **R** type is for Whorehouses® like the type we grew up in.

Yep! Mwah… The men doing us young Junior Sissy Whores, JSW® were trained how to have sex with Sissy kids so the children aren't abused or get hurt when they perform sex-training.

Well, fine! Mwah… I guess I get the Whoring-Station® and Whorehouse® rules thing.

Jane the Whorehouse (WH) rules are all a little different. Like Whoring-Stations are used to service the general population of workers by Associate (ASW), Professional (PSW) and Certified (CSW) Sissy-Whores. Although CSW usually work in L-Type, high-class, upscale clientele Whoring-Stations.

Huh! Did you get that out of the Sissy Manual? Mwah…

Mwah… Heee... heee... Yes! In fact I did, SM069, Section [7]. You should read it sometime Jane! Poke... Poke... Poke... hee... hee... Mwah… I love you Jane!

[2.17] STUDBUCKS

One hour later after fulfilling obligations…

That's it for me. My bellies full of Man-Cream®.

Yeah me too Mary, besides we're gonna get plenty dudes during, our Whorehouse hours. I love the flavored dick-milk they have here at **Studbucks**®.

Yeah, I had the Mocha-Jizz.

I had the Spermy-Latte. Umm...umm! Yummy!

[2.18] RELATIONSHIP

The Gurls discuss their devotion to each other...

Did you see any Sissies we know?

Yeah when you went to douche-out a DOM-Bitch® couple from Sissyology class were taking penetrations a few benches away from where we were. We all said hi, I got the Bitch's WeeeChat and her DOM just looked at me with that, *get the fuck away from my bitch*, look. Geeezzz... She was a hot looking Bitch, (Jane rubs her clit and squirts out a load thinking about her). Aaaaagh! Ouch! Mary!

Jane! Remember what I told you about me tightening your leash?

Yes, Mistress Mary! Ow! (Mary lightly elbows Jane). Jizz-Us!

Huh! Jane, I'm just trying to define our obligations to each other.

Ow! Mary someday you're gonna break a rib elbowing me like that. I have the body of a seven year old little kid and sometimes I think you forget how tiny I am.

Sorry Baby. Hmm... Kiss... But you know I get jealous.

Talk about domination issues! I spoke with Nicky and some other Sissy DOM friends. They all told me I'm too loose with you Jane.

Mary! Really? They're just jealous of us! They know we're in love, it's obvious. And because we don't follow the stupid Sissy DOM-Bitch paradigm of Master-Slave they want to start trouble between us. They resent us!

Well, they said they noticed you wear your Bitch collar I put around your precious little neck but they never see you on a leash.

So what Mare! Huh! Really, they're just jealous!

They never see me disciplining you in front of them either. The other DOM Gurls think you're just a wild little Hoe on the loose, no control, no Bitch training. They've never seen me, pissing on you or slapping you for not obeying me! Sniff... sniff...

Cum on Mare!

Sniff... They said you don't respect me! Sniff... sniff, and someday, sniff... sniff, you'll just run away from me oooh! Aaagh! Huh... Sniff, and leave me... Bitchless! Huh, huh, huh... (Mary is having a melt-down).

Mary! Hey, (Jane hugs her Lover and partner) Mary? You know I listen to you and you know I love you. Hey! Who sleeps in your arms and I take your love cream up my Sissy snatch every night. I'm Sissy-Promised® to you Mary! I'm always there for you. Cause I love you. Sniff... Sniff...

Sniff... Yeah Jane! I know, but they say such mean things to me about you. Like if I don't put you in your place, she's going to leave you and stupid stuff like that! Aaaagh... Huh.... Sniff....

Hey you're never going to lose me! We're Sissy-Promised to each other and we're going to get Sissy-Married, we're life-partners! I'm not going anywhere without you my friend. I want to be with you forever!

Sniff... Sniff... I know Jane. We're in love with each other. And you know I've never hit you or been mean to you ever. I would never treat you like they treat their Bitches. They yank on their leashes like they're dogs or something. Then while their Bitch sucks their Cockettes they piss on them and slap them in the face just to humiliate them in public, they're so abusive it makes me sick. Sniff...

Well most Bitches are abused by their DOMs. And most DOMs have more than one Bitch. Hell, over sixty-nine percent of Promised couples never get married. You're listening to your friends like they know what they're doing!

No! Jane you know I don't follow their advice.

Well huh! Is this what you want Mary? Do you want to abuse me and treat me like a piece of shit like the other Sissy DOMs treat their Bitches?

NO! NO! Jane I would never treat you like that or hurt you! You're a free Bitch not a slave. You know I'm your DOM and you wear my collar. I'm in control only because I love you and try to make the right decisions for both of us. Hell, I bought your leash and I've never even used it on you. I'm not into treating you like you're my lapdog or telling you how to behave yourself. Jane, you're not bellicose like a human we're a peace loving Sissy couple.

Hmm... Hmm... Yeah you did put the leash on me once. Hmmm… Remember, we were in bed and I was acting like a puppy with the leash in my mouth and wanted you to spank my ass and kidding around you put the leash on me.

Yeah, yeah... Huh! Sure Honey, I remember. Hmm... Kisss... But that was role playing Okay, we both had fun and the Sissy-Sex we had was awesome. Kisss... But I didn't yank on your leash, I gently took you by your leash and you followed me into the hot-tub. This wasn't cruelty it's Sissy love making.

Yeah lover. Hmm... Kisss.... Okay! Well hey, I do listen to you Mary. I know I joke around and have fun with you but I'm obedient to you whether you realize it or not.

I know Jane. Mwah...

When you say, hey Jane, blow-me! Or, when you say, hey let's go to the Whoring-Station and get screwed because our cunts are empty. Or, hey Honey, get your ass in bed and make love to me. I'm there, I always obey you Baby!

Haa... haaa... hee... Yeah Jane! It only proves you listen to me when you want sex. And hey, you're the only Bitch for me Babe. I'll never have other Bitches, just you Honey. I'm a one Bitch kind of DOM. Hmmm... Mwah... Hmmm... never let me go Baby. Mwah...

[2.19] DATING

Note: skip this part if you hate mushy stuff

But Jane, when I tell you I have a date with a really nice Stud® guy and I expect you to stay home and wait-up for me. I expect you to greet me at the door when I get home. And maybe be dressed in a really sexy lingerie-set, like one of those cute maid outfits I bought for you. And at my feet begging me to forgive you for not being a better Bitch. But instead of being the loving faithful Bitch I'm Promised too, sometimes you just go out to an illegal Non-Stud gentlemen's club to take an **FO**® [16.7]. So you don't listen all the time Jane.

Mare! Well yeah, I know I'm a tramp and you're a smart beautiful Lady. But we're two different kinds of people. You're an elegant sophisticated sexy, very attractive intelligent classy Lady, I'm a Hoe! I'm a Sissy Hoe, and I LOVE SEX! You know that, you know I was bred a Bitch and need way more dick than a DOM like you.

Yes, yes, I know! You don't have to remind me, Jane.

And Mary, I go out on you because I like to and also need to. I'm never going to be as knock-out beautiful as you are. Just face it. I'm just your gang-banging scanky Sissy Bitch. And you're never going to be like me. You have sex till you get that filled-up feeling then you're over it, you're ready to turn the red light off and close the Whorehouse® door. Me, I screw till all the nut-sacks are empty. And I don't even care if they're Non-Stud men or Studs! To me a dick's a dick!

Sniff... sniff... Aaaah!

What? Mary, what the hell you crying about now for? God-of-Cocks! You're such a drama queen.

Sniff... yeah... sniff... I remember when I used to get home from a romantic date with some really handsome Stud dude back in high school and you wouldn't be there waiting up for me! Huh, huh... Sniff... Sniff... how do you think I felt Jane?

Huh! I wasn't on a date, I can tell you that!

How do you think I felt when I spent the rest of the night by the phone waiting to hear a call from a hospital or from some asshole at a Non-Stud club telling me how he read my contact info off the tag on your collar and to cum and fetch my Bitch off the floor cause they're closing up for the night.

Huh! I must have had a goodtime!

Or if I didn't get a call, I'm sitting there crying all night wondering if you're lying in a pool of cum in some alley screwed into an orgasmic convolution. How do you think I felt Jane? Aaah... aaah ha... haa! Sniff sometimes I feel like you don't even love me anymore! Aaah... aaah ha...

Oh Geeez! Mary you like going out and making love to Stud dudes don't you? Have you ever thought how you made me feel when you'd invite me over to your place for a sleep-over and you'd just leave me there to make-out with your Mom and Dad and end up making love with them! Because you'd go out on dates with Studs, did it ever occur to you maybe I'd be jealous?

Mare, you'd cum home from these dates and always be so amazed how the Stud was so polite to you. He'd open doors and was a real gentleman. Treated you like a Stud Lady and made you feel special. The more you boasted the more I wanted to throw-up a wad of you daddy's load!

Wow! Talk about over dramatization! Jane, you loved sleeping with my parents.

Yeah true! But, when we go anywhere or we just enter a classroom, all the big handsome Stud dudes swarm around you taking photos with you and I'm there! Just your little Sissy Bitch Gurlfriend following you around, standing there being ignored and pushed out of the way by all of your admirers.

Okay, okay... So I like when big strong Stud men treat me nice. It proves to us, Sissy-Ladies are treated just as nice as human Stud-Ladies. I feel vindicated because I'm a beautiful women and I'm treated like one regardless of whether I'm a Sissy or not. And regardless of the fact, that I was created by scientists to be sexually abused by men to bring peace to this world!

Great Mary! I'm proud of you and I think Sissydom® should give you a medal for having big enough balls to have those macho Stud assholes beg for your Sissy cooch. Bravo! You're the Queen of Sissies! (Jane mocks Mary's justification). Woo hooo! Yah! Haa... haaa.... haaaa....

Yeah very funny Jane! I'm the queen alright. Huh, huh, huh... Sniff... Sniff... I'm HORRIBLE!

Whoa! Honey I was joking!

I'm destroying a beautiful relationship with the one person I love more than I love myself! You mean everything to me Jane. Okay, that's it. I'll stop dating Studs! Jane, I love you and I'm not going to let anything or anyone cum between us. Studs are off my list.

Mary wait, wait. Hey I don't want you to give up dating Studs, it's something you really like doing. Just like I don't wanna give up taking an FO. I love you too and I'm happy for you! When you cum home from a date and you're super happy and telling me some colorful story. How the Stud took you to a nice restaurant, great show then you went back to his place. Wine and romantic candle lit moments and you both made passionate love together. I'm always happy you had a nice time. Sure I mean I feel like you broke my heart, but hey, I'd do or suffer anything for your happiness Mary.

Oh Jane! Mwah… Why didn't you tell me how you felt?

Mwah… Because Mary, in the Sissy Promise rules, it's not considered cheating when a Sissy DOM dates a Stud. I'm not as naïve about our relationship as you think I am.

Jane I don't give-a-shit about the stupid rules, I love you! I don't wanna break your heart! I care about how you feel!

Mary I did tell you how I felt, but you weren't listening.

When did you tell me that Jane?

When I wasn't there when you got home from your Stud dates back in high school. When I went out and got laid without you. That was the writing on the wall Mary. And I don't care what your asshole DOM friends tell you about me being a Hoe!

I'll go with you. I'll go to those shithole gentlemen clubs. Snifff… I'll do whatever you want. Sniff… I'll do anything for you! Snifff…

Mary, it's cheating when you go out on me! I don't care if the other Sissy Bitches don't have the balls to say or do anything about how they're abused by their DOM! Mary, we have equality in our relationship, we treat each other with respect for one another. Unlike my peers, I'm a free Bitch! And we don't need to behave the way the other Promised DOM-Bitch pairs do. We have something they don't.

Snifff… What Jane?

We love each other sweetheart!

Oooh! Jane, I love you so much. (They lovingly embrace) Hmmm... kisss... kiss... I'll never cheat on you again Sweetheart.

[2.20] HEADING BACK

Gurls head back to their dorm WH069S...

Cum-on, let's hurry back to our dorm, it's already six-o-nine and we have to setup and open the dorm door of our Whorehouse at eight o'clock. This is perfect! We can do training while we study.

Sounds like a plan Mary my sexy Sissy-Lady.

You mean your soon-to-be DOM-Bitch® marriage partner?

Of course if you say so Mary, after all, you're the one with the bigger clit.

That's right my Wildflower Sissy-Gurl, I have bigger tits, balls and an enormous three-inch Cocklette®, so don't forget it Bitch. You wear the collar. I'm the one with the leash in this Sissy Family!

Ooooh! I'm scared Mary! Uoooh! Are you gonna spank me? (Jane jokingly sucks her thumb like a child).

Spank! (Mary gives Jane a spank on her ass).

Ooooh! Daddy more spankings! (Jane speaking in a baby voice) Give me more Daddy pleeeease... I've been a bad Bitch!

Yes you are a bad Sissy-Gurl! Spank!

Yeah, I'm bad Daddy, poke me with your big three-incher!

Jane, you're going to make the perfect Sissy-Wife. Mwah…

Restricted-Student WH planning…

Mwah… Hey! Tonight let's set up our holes in doggie-style for the horny boys so we can hit the books. Because I can't read a book in missionary position.

Yeah Mare, I'm going to love taking man-meat while absorbing all this Sissyology stuff. And in class, when Rim Me started talking about the **PWP**® rule number six, where the Studs with a higher social status only do compensation with branded **Pimped-Whores**® from a Harem.

Yeah sounds good, I'd like to screw somebody worth a lot of money someday! And my dad gave me some Gurly advice about sizes. Mwah…

Hmmm… What do you and your Dad compare Stud-Cock® notes? Haaa ha… Mwah…

Yes we do! In fact he told me the rule-of-thumb is, the wealthier the dude the longer the cock because the (L12) dosage **PED**® [4.D-G1.11] meds to grow a twelve-incher is really expensive. Men get measured by wealth first, than a dosage is prescribed to regulate the length. This is why my Dad told me to always check the dudes **SCR** [5.E2.1] score before you bed down with him.

Uuuuh! Oooh! Yeah, I popped a load. Dam! I'm still turned on about the **FEM**® lecture today. I filled a Clit-Sock® during the lecture about FEM-Cream in the Sex Psychology class. It was so erotic. Oooh! That felt good! Mwah…

Mwah… Yeah, I was having these little **Sissy-Gasms** in my Vaganus® just thinking about the FEM penis size being sixteen point nine inches long and three inches wide. Simply amazing!

Mwah… I love it! When do I get to meet one of these world record sized dicks? I was salivating thinking about having a massive member of a FEM up my cooch. Haa... Haaa… haaa...

Yeah! Well, neither of us is a branded Sissy cunt so the only place we could get big monster sized penises would be at a horse stud farm like the ones we visited during our **Whore**® training at **JAS**® camp. Mwah…

Yeah, yeah… The lecture was super interesting, but right now I'd settle for any good old eight-incher. Mwah…

Mwah… I hear you Gurlfriend! I'm itching for a good cunt stuffing tonight too. We got it made baby! Mwah…

Mwah… Yep! While we study Jane! I'm not going to let you fall behind in your studies just because we're still obligated to open our Whorehouse door for duty between eight and midnight like we did back home. This is college and we're going to get through it together.

Yes, Ma'am! (Jane salutes). Mwah…

Jane, I'm not kidding! I'm not going to let you drop-out and go to work as a common Hoe at some Whoring-Station like Annie! I didn't make my Sissy-Promise to you just to see you throw your life away!

Yes, Mary… (Jane says in a deep tone of a pacifying voice). Kiss… I know and I love you too. Mary who's ring is this on my finger? (Jane holds her ring finger up and wiggles it in front of Mary's face).

Yes! It's the one I put on your finger in the park. Sniff... sniffle.

 Is this what you wanted to hear Mary? Do you want to hear me telling you how much I love you continually twenty-four seven? If that's the case? I will. Because you mean everything to me Mary, all I look forward to everyday is waking up in your arms.

I love you too Jane, sniff... sniff. Mwah…

Mwah… Yes, just keep telling me you love me. It's all I want sweetheart! Kiss... (They're both drama queens, as they hug and kiss each other). Let's go! Cum-on!

Hey Mare! Just a reminder. This is your engagement bow on my clit, I love you and I'm wearing your collar so don't forget it Lover. Kisss…

[2.21] WH DUTY

Doing cum-munity service at WH069…

Here we are the senior dorm hall. Wow! What the heck is going on here? (There's a line a college dudes that wraps from their door all the way around the dorm hall building).

Hey Mick! Hey James! Mwah… Mwah… Wow! What a line!

Yeah James! Mwah… I told everybody about how you guys are the best Sissy Hoes and they told all their friends. And wow! Your **SissyTube**® video went viral!

Whoa! There's got to be at least six hundred ninety Studs in line to be serviced!

Oh, we've been in line waiting for you for hours so we could mount your fine pussies before your cunts got too sloppy.

Oh really? Well, don't worry Mick. We strictly follow all the American National Standards Institutes (ANSI) standards for Whorehouse® protocols, also the **OSHA®** [23.34] safety regulations as well. We both douche-out and PrettyPuss® test every sixty-nine loads so you Studs can have a nice fresh clean Vaganus® when you do get your chance at our pretty little love-holes. Oh and the MSDS manual is available at each **LCB®** pertaining to the penetration orifice cleaning and lubricating products we use. Workplace hazards is an issue.

Huh! You Gurls manage Orifice Safety and supply Pussy? Wow!

Well anyway! Give me and my Sissy-Bitch Fiancée here a few minutes to get everything ready. You guys know we open at eight o'clock, give or take sixty-nine seconds, right?

Yeah, yeah… Sure! Standard hours for a Restricted Student (RS) type Whorehouse®.

Right! So it's only a Whorehouse not a Whoring-Station so we're not open 24 hours and its not full service.

Sure, sure… Mary, no problem we understand it's a student S type so no blow-jobs while you guys study.

Mwah… Yeah, well, I just wanted you to be sure about what to expect.

The Gurls setup their dorm whorehouse WH069S...

Hey Jane! Can you help me slide my labor compensation bench, the LCB® over to yours so we can study together? And we'll need to lock it down. You know these Stud boys are animals.

Yep! There it's clipped into the floor Babe for safety proposes. I filled the lubrication dispensers, turned on the video system and all the monitors are on playing a sixty-nine minute loop of us being gangbanged.

Perfect Honey! Mwah… You're the best partner. Mwah… You ready? It's time to open up for business.

You mean training? (Jane says with a stern face).

Haa haaa… Yes! My Sissy-Lover open the brothels door for sex training, my cunt is aching to be filled with man-meat.

Hey Mary?

What Jane?

You called me your Fiancée before when we were talking to James and Mick.

Huh! Yeah so?

Kiss… I liked it. You made me feel special. Mwah…

Mwah… Oooh sweetheart! Hold me kisss... I can't wait to be married to you Jane. Let's tell our folks when we're home on winter break? Okay! Mwah…

Eight o'clock…..

Well, cum on in boys. Stroke those Stud pricks and get them ready to pop a load. Cum on in boys Mary and I both need a good pounding. We're open Monday through Friday, but check the WH069S schedule online for notices. And Boy's try not to take all night to cum in us! There's a long line of you Studs and it wouldn't be right for the others if you take forever to finish your business.

Thursday night at midnight…..

Is it midnight yet Jane?

Yeah Mary! Closing time. Last call for dick! Whooohooo!

Okay, then these boys are the last ones for the night. After these Studs pull out of us, I'll turn the red Whorehouse® light off and locking the door.

Mary, be merciful! There's still about six or nine boys in the waiting area and another sixty-nine in the hall outside.

Jane we got class in the morning my little Wildflower. Besides we have the NSA® meeting. These boys are just gonna have to jerk-off or cum back tomorrow night. Wait I think we have to close the WH tomorrow because the NSA meeting might last into the evening.

Oh yeah! The NSA meeting with the two old ladies.

Well anyway, we can't service the entire male student body in one night. Those are the RS rules.

Aaaagh! Thanks for the load dude. Okay Mary, he was the last one. Close it up, we did our duty. Ahhhh… Okay doors locked! (Jane shouts).

Great! Let's douche-out and jump in bed, my cunts exhausted. Me and you Babe. Mwah… We sure know how to run a Whorehouse. Ummm… Kiss... Mwah… Love you.

[2.22] FRIDAY

Friday morning...

Cum-on Jane! For-fuck-sake! We'll be late, stop sucking on me. Mwah… I really don't need any more blow-jobs, let's go.

Huh! Last load Mare! Gak…. Gek… Guk… (Jane swallows Mary's Cocklette and balls then chokes). Glrck…

Okay last one! Ahhh… Here Jane, swallow this Bitch! Aaaaagh! Aaagh! Aaagh...

Glrck… Blahhh! Aaagh! Blahhh! Ahhh! Geeez! (Jane up chucks Mary's wad and breakfast).

JANE! You just throw-up all over our brand new silk sheets! Dang-it Gurl! What a mess!

Whoops! Sorry Mare! I guess I can't handle a Sissy-Poop® breakfast out of your ass and a huge cum wade at the same time.

Well yeah Jane you should take a break once in a while! I know you love the sweet Sissy-Poop® out of my ass but Geeezz… Slow down Gurl. God-of-Cocks what a mess! I'll lick it up!

No Jane! We're gonna be late for math class.

Wow! My favorite! (Jane says sarcastically).

Yeah I know my little wild Gurl. But it's required so suck it up. After math class we do lunch milking, then Vaganus Economics 101, then the **NSA**® meeting with Yaoi and Rimme.

And the name, Rim Me, it's not suggestive at all is it? Haaa haa… No, nothing implied here!

Yeah, yeah… Our favorite old ladies!

They don't look old, they just dress old fashion.

Hmmm… You're right now that I think about it. Both have those perfect beautiful Amazon bodies. Tall with beautiful long legs, perfect complexion, stacked and awesome bottoms.

Hey Jane if we can score a scholarship from the NSA, I'll kiss their bottoms. I'm like all in! Whatever it takes!

Oooh yeah! Sure Mary, we've kissed plenty of female asses. In fact, I'm sure we've bedded down with every instructor we've ever had.

Huh! Yeah, for academic purposes only! Heee he hee… But you know the best female back-door holes I've had have been our beautiful Sissy-Breeding Moms.

Heee heeee… Yeah! Our Moms are cool!

Right! Talking about loveholes, it's one of the few things I miss about being away from home, not being able to eat out my Mommy's baby-maker.

Yeah I love licking and kissing my Mom's vagina too especially seeing how it's the hole I came out of. Yeah our Moms have sweet mommy holes! The best part is when all us gurl-girls go to bed together, munching on our cunts, suckling our clits and fisting each other all night.

Oh yeah! I love eating out your Mom. Mrs. Dune has the sweetest Mommy hole.

Yeah, I love eating-out your Mom too Jane.

Our moms have the sweetest cunts. I guess it's why they were chosen by the Cockolic church to be Priest Service Nuns, **PSN**® [9.I2.9.n].

Right, right. I'm so glad both our families are religious. Our Nun Mommy's sleep with Priests and take Holy-Cream® up their Blessed ass-pussies. Then our Mom's go home and our Daddy's eat the Holy-Cream out of their Nun-Wives. Our Moms are the coolest!

But Yaoi and Rimme, hmmm? I just don't see that happening. I mean sure, they're so fashion-model beautiful, I would love to bed-down with either one of them. But I just feel like we're not going to get the chance to lick any female clits today. Besides, I bet Yaoi and Rimme have sex with plenty of gorgeous handsome men.

Huh! Maybe, but I doubt it Mare! I mean our Mother's walk around in mini-skirts and their tits are all over the place and Yaoi and Rimme, well I just don't see this turning into anything but a formal business relationship with two, stuffy, super conservative, book-worm, prudish, lady Professors. And like you said, they probably have a whole entourage of attractive men following them around.

[2.23] AFTER CLASS

Well, we made it through another exciting day at college Gurlfriend.

Yep! And I think I have a brain aneurism from math class. Haa haaa… But the good news is part in the Vaganus Economics class was super interest. The pay scales of the different Professional Sissies Whores was fascinating.

Yeah, pay rates for, Common Hoe, Associate, Branded, Certified Professionals and Free-Whores.

Geeezz… I didn't know there were that many types of Whores!

I know my heads spinning! The Branded Whores make the most money.

Oh yeah! By far, they make six point nine times more than the next highest, the Certified. Plus all their expenses are paid for by the US Department of Commerce. Sweet deal!

So, you ready for this? (Mary asks as they approach the office door).

Yeah, yeah! Honey, but hold my hand please. Mwah…

Oh Jane! Cum-on? We have nothing to worry about. You know for a Wildflower who screws like a rabbit, you sure are timid around these big bosomed female Professor Ladies?

Yes Mommy (Jane has her thumb in her mouth mocking Mary's parental advice). Just because I wanna suckle their big titties, there's no need for concern!

Jane! What am I gonna to do with you? Mwah…

[2.24] NSA

The National Sissydom Association (NSA) meeting…

Knock, knock.

Oh Gurls! Yes! Cum in, cum in. We've been expecting you. You know my colleague Professor Rim Me.

Hi Professors! Oh Professor Rim Me, we're still ingesting all the information about the secretive FEM ladies we learned about in your lecture. It was so exciting!

Haa ha... ha... hee... Well, Gurls I'm just glad it was fascinating enough to swallow instead of barfing it up. Haa... hee... haa…

Tea Gurls?

Yes Professor. Oh, definitely. Sip… (Mary sips the tea). Ummm… Yummy tea Professor. It has a sweet cummy flavor. Jane and I both found your class (sip...sip...sip) sooo interesting and would like to learn more.

Thank you Mary. Please sit down both of you, get comfortable we have so much to talk to you about. Sip…

Ahhh! Great tea Professor, semen favored is my favorite! (Jane exclaims). Ummm…

Yes Jane, we knew you Gurls would appreciate the cummy flavor. Well, about the FEM ladies I feel you'll be learning all about FEMs very, very soon and in an unexpected way.

Huh? (Jane questions the response). But Professor didn't you say we don't know much about the FEMs?

Yeah... But, sip... sip... I happen to have this really close friend who I've been in-and-out of bed with (Yaoi looks over at Rimme and winks). Who keeps me in-the-loop and informed about their secret religious society.

Ooooh! A secret society! (Both Gurls eyes light-up and they stare at each other in suspense).

Well Gurls, I'll tell you a secret, but this is just between us so don't go spreading rumors around about the FEM ladies.

Oooh! We would never tell anyone Professor. Please, please tell us more! (The Gurls are all a glee with the thought of knowing more about FEM women).

Well, you're all excited, sip... sip... sip, but Gurls I'm serious this is not to leave this room. (The Gurls move closer to the Professors). I heard the FEM ladies choose only beautiful Sissy-Gurls like you two, young proud Sissies, Breed from long lines of Sissies.

Ohhhh! (The Gurls are surprised yet apprehensive and move slightly away from the Professors).

There's even talk about there being two FEMs who teach here at FUCIT. I mean, who would have thought? FEMs here!

Seriously! (Jane jumps up and shouts). I'd love to get to meet their endowments hee heee... If you know what I mean? (Jane winks at Yaoi). Sip... sip... sip... Uoooh! Strong tea Professor.

Yes of course you would Jane. I know exactly what you mean and fortunately for you Gurls, I have a feeling I can arrange that special intimate meeting.

Wow! Intimate! Awesome thank you Professor. Aaagh! Whoops! I squirted, sorry. (Jane has a small Sissygasm and ejaculates a small wad which she catches in her hand and swallows like nothing happened). Gulp!

With FEM Ladies? Wow! And it was so exciting to hear you tell us about their huge penises! Sip... sip... sip...

Ooooh! Aaaagh! Whoops! Sorry! I squirted on your dress Professor. (Jane pops off again with no sock on).

It's fine Jane, after all I have a PhD in Sissyology and I fully understand B-Type Gurls like you abruptly have orgasms for no particular reason.

So you Gurls are from the same, sip... sip... town up state?

Yes, we grew up together in MO-Town, New Jerksey, went sip... sip... to the same schools, same JAS summer camps, lived just a few houses away from each, sip... other all of our lives. Sip... (More tea sipping). And now we're roommates here on campus. Ummm... Whoa! This is powerful tea. (Mary is getting a little dizzy). Sip...

Well, you must have a wonderful friendship?

Yes, we do, Mary and I are Sissy-Promised to each other... Sip... Sip...

Yes, I see the Promised in the personal information section of your records.

And we're planning on being Sissy married soon. Mwah... (The Gurls kiss).

Yes Jane, I noticed the pink engagement bow on your clit, how sweet. I wish the best for both of you. Well Gurls, I have good news for both of you. Professor Rim Me and I have reviewed both of your scholastic and public records extensively and we both approved the NSA membership, scholarship and internship for both of you.

Oooh! Oh my Cock-God! Thank you, Thank you both. It would be an honor to be in the NSA program! Ooooh! (Jane pops another Sissygasm load in her special place). Oooh!

Gurls it's because of your meritorious efforts, I mean your records show both of you have shown a strong determination to serve the public. And we feel the NSA internship positions and scholarships can be a spring board for you to enter into public service in your near futures... sip... sip. And Sissies who do an internship with the NSA often go on to careers in, politics, public administration or law.

Oooh! We're sooo grateful Professors! Thank you.

Well one other thing caught our attention Gurls. We also browsed your family histories as well and I noticed both of your mothers have taken up vows as Priest Service Nuns, PSN in the, Holy Order of the Blessed Sisters of Priests at the, Blessed Sissy Lady of Cock-Whores Church.

Yes they've both... sip... sip... received the Holy Sacrament of Sissy-Breeder® their Cum-firmation® and also had their bottoms blessed by the Holy Cockolic Church.

Ah huh, they did. Sip… sip… Ahhh! Wow!

What's wrong my Dear? (Yaoi asks).

Nothing, I just felt a dizzy feeling cum over me. So they can both take the Holy Sacrament of **Cum-Union**® in their douched-out ass-pussies.

Yeah and then, our mothers qualified to take their vows and be cum Priest Service Nuns, they're both PSN Ladies now. Sip… Sip… Whoa! Professors, you sure this is just tea? Because it has a punch. Hmmm…. It reminds me of the stuff Father Tom would give Mary and I after mass when me were Altar-Gurls.

Yeah, yeah! It has the same effect and taste. I mean, I'm feeling a little tippy here. And if I recall, Father Tom would visit us in the vestibules Gurls changing room and have his way with us.

Yeah! I'm sure it was where we both received out first Holy Cum-Union, in the back of the Church. And we were sooo little at the time I'm sure we ended up wearing most of Father Tom's Cum-Union. Uooooh…. My head. (Jane and Mary are both holding their heads while wondering what's happening). Sip…

These stories about the Cockolic Church sounds very interesting. Tell me more about you mother Jane? (Rimme asks).

Yes, Ooooh! I'm feeling a little dizzy too… Ooooh! But yeah, every Sunday night Father Tom beds them both down to service his ordained manhood and to do penance for all their sins by receives Holy Ordained Cream.

I see. This would account for why the two of you practice **Cockolicism**® [9.B.3]. Being followers ourselves, Professor Rimme and I have noticed you both attending mass in our local Cockolic Church near campus.

Oh! You're Cockolic! Well that would explain your conservative appearances. But yeah, Our Moms sin so much and have so many un-clean thoughts about Stud men it takes them all night to do their penance. So they both usually sleep with Father Tom and some of the other Priests on Sunday night.

Well such religious devotion in your families is good news. You see Gurls, Professor Rimme and I are also both very religious and devote Cockolics. Oh and we're FEM Cardinals of the Holy Cockolic Church.

WHAT? (The Gurls are fading fast as the FEM-Cream laced tea is taking effect). Jane! Jane!

Huuuh...!!!... (Both Gurls are slipping into unconsciousness from a sacred blend of several drops of blessed sperm). Whoa! Professor! Holy-Poop! You're a freaken Femmm...?

Mare! I think this Tea is making meeeeeee....

I can't move Jane! What's happening? Aaaah, I'm dizzy!

Femsss... Mare.... Aaaah...

Jane! I... love.... uuu...

I... looove... uuuu... toooooooo... Marrrr... eeeee...

Revised version of this section can be found in EN14, FLASHBACK Editor's Note: NSA meeting, EN03...

Chapter: 3 Inoculation

[3.1] PREP

Inoculation preparation…

Cardinal **Rimme**, their lights are out.

Good job Archbishop **Yaoi**, Thank you for Jizzing up their tea for us. Kisss… (The Pimp ladies are very intimate with each other).

Well it was an easy potion to whip up. six drops of Pope-Sperm®, nine drops from a Cock Illuminati Supreme Grand Exalted Master, Level 69, six drops from a Dwarf American Toad and finally nine drops of Dali-Cream® and Walla! They didn't know what hit them. Mwah…

Excellent as usual, Yaoi. Mwah…

Mwah… Cardinal, they'll remember only small fragments of the next 48 hours, when they're delivered to their dorm Sunday afternoon.

Okay, but make sure they have all the pain relief they need. I don't want these Sissy-Gurls feeling any discomfort or have the impression they were abused. And make sure bouquets of flowers are sent to their dorm on Sunday.

Yes, Cardinal Rimme. Mwah…

Well Yaoi, let's get these two love birds to the Inoculation Chamber for the **Bitchification**® ritual [8.H1].

Sure, I'll call down to our Pimped-Nun team in the inoculation chamber.

Yes! And why don't you open the bookshelf entryway to the catacombs for the preparation team. They'll be here to bring the Gurls down into the FUCIT Cathedral.

And Cardinal Rimme, my dear colleague, I wanted to share something with you. There's talk amongst the Holy-Pimps.

Well, what are the Pimps talking about now Yaoi?

They're talking about these young budding Sissies we've so meticulously selected. I hear they're discussing nominating the Gurls to have an audience with our Holy Cock-Pope® in Rome for a Papal Blessing with his Holy-Cream.

Seriously Pimp Yaoi! I mean we haven't even branded them yet! An audience with our Holy Cock-Pope! Really now. And yes I do think these pretty little Sissy flowers are blooming, but seriously. Let's not interrupt the process.

Yes Cardinal Rimme, besides we haven't Rosebudded their unblessed bottoms yet.

Right, right… Let's just go down to the chamber and get ready to penetrate them in the presence of the Holy Conclave of Pimps.

Yes we need to hose these chosen ones in their special places with our Holy **Love-Cream**® making them our obedient faithful followers first. And once we have inoculated and branded them they'll be in the, Holy Order of the Blessed Sisters of Pimps, and under our command.

Hmmm… Under our command? Pimp Yaoi, you mean under our Holy Guidance?

Yes I'm sorry, Cardinal Rimme, of course, under our Holy Guidance. And I believe Jane and Mary could be a problem if we try to split them up.

Yes, couldn't agree more with you Yaoi.

My Excellence, with the DOM Mary belonging to you Cardinal Rimme and the Bitch Jane being in my Whore-Nun Harem. We can get into all kinds of trouble with the, US Department of Sissy Justice if we keep them apart.

Yes, especially because they're **Sissy-Promised**® [6.F.A] to each other. And don't forget, they're also a DOM-Bitch Bonded Pair **DBBP** [2.B2.13]. It's forbidden by the HCC [9] to violate the Promise and or the Bond which binds their love for one another.

Absolutely! Well we could setup an Inter-Harem Trade Agreement, an **IHTA**® [9.I2.9.o] which has the two always in one harem or the other.

Right, so at any one time we'll have one of them who belongs to our Harem and one who is a guest immigrant-whore. We just bounce them back and forth between our two Harems. Huh! It sounds like a **Choosey-Susie**® [8.H2.4]. Haaa haa…

Haa ha… Very funny, except for one detail, our Gurls are purebred Sissies not prostitutes. So to keep a low profile on this pair I suggest we keep the US Department of Commerce, Sissy Trade Division (STD) from meddling where it doesn't belong.

Yes and not to mention flying under the radar of the Intern Revenue Service, the **IRS** [23.59]. Because the IHTA would fall under the auspices of the **NAFTA** [23.32]. Right, the National Anal Free Trade Agreement.

Yep it's pretty much the way the big corporations did it, they sent the American jobs overseas then screwed the US government out of the taxes and nobodies the wiser. It's fascism at its best. Exactly and call it Fascism, Studism, Globalism, the NAFTA lets us legally, evade, avoid and escape from paying taxes when we penetrate their **Vaganus**®.

Well regardless of the politics involved, this especially is a problem because these two are a BSP.

Right! Bonded Sissy Pair, Jane and Mary are a **BSP**®. The Sissy Breeding Program (SBP) made plans for these two before they were even born. And the SBP under the guidance of the HCC ordered their mothers to carry-out the bonding procedures on the two of them at a very early age.

Yes Cardinal, which obviously turned out to be very successful judging by how they're joined at the hip emotionally to one another in a symbiotic relationship?

Right, there's nothing coincidental about Jane and Mary.

Pimp Yaoi, I'm much more concerned about the threatening emails I'm receiving from members of the Cock-Illuminati, the **CI**© [23.16.2]. They wanting to schedule these soon to be newly branded Pimped-Whore® Nuns, these PWN Gurls to service their sexual needs or else. I tried to explain to them, Jane and Mary are just young freshmen here at college. And they can't just be flown all over the world for a one night gangbang for their CI Grand-Masters.

And besides, Mary and Jane haven't been chosen just to be pimped to everyone in the Cock-Illuminati. These Sissies are special. I mean they're more than just Whores. Their whole lives have been planned from cradle to the grave. The Holy Cockolic Church was instrumental in creating this Sissy pair and I'm not going to let a bunch of **CI**© playboys mess with the Church sponsored One Cock World Order, the **OCWO** [9.B.1].

But Cardinal Rimme, why does the Cock-Illuminati suddenly need to have these two PWN Gurls specifically? There're other more experienced Nuns to choose from?

Because, they got word Jane has the highest **Cockage**® [7.G5.4] of any Sissy her age! She's also the youngest Sissy to ever be chosen to be pimped. And to make things worse a photo of Mary was sent to all the CI and they feel Mary is so gorgeously beautiful she should be nominated to be our Holy Cock-Popes Vestal Bitch.

Jizzz-Us! [9.I3.0]. What-the-fuck has gotten into these pricks!

Yes I agree. Besides, these two Sissies are even more special having had FEM history in their family's cock-lineage.

Yes, yes, I know but they have responsibilities here on campus. They have school work and also as Branded Pimped-Whore® Nuns of the HCC, I mean, Jizz-Us! My dick doesn't suck itself!

Hmmm... Cardinal this is an urgent matter; we need to have the cooperation of the Cock-Illuminati to maintain the balance between our Secret Holy Order of Pimps and the United States Cunt-gress.

Yes, I agree Yaoi, the members of the CI are all Grand Master Cocks of the HCC. Without them the HCC would lose some but not all of its persuasive political and financial power here in the United States Inc. The Corporatocracy must remain stable.

Well, the HCC is the world's oldest and largest financial entity and has most if not all, control over the United States Inc. government. But like you said, we still need the Cock-Illuminati to maintain a balance between the US government and business.

Of course, if the HCC is to implement the new, One Cock World Order to accomplish total penetration of the Working Class here in the USA Inc. and then go on to complete,

World Cock domination through, Vaganus ad-dick-tion

Pimp Yaoi, I agree whole heartedly. The USA Inc. is a business not a Cunt-tree. And their ambitious plan to implant a **Vaganus**® in every home in the world is genius. And not to cut this conversation short, but for now we better get moving. It takes a half an hour to go down through the FUCIT catacombs beneath the Sissyology building to the FUCIT Cathedrals Inoculation chamber.

God-of-Cocks! Do you think next time they build a HCC Cathedral they could install a god-dam elevator?

Sure Rimme. Just send a memo to the Cock-Pope® and maybe you'll get your miracle. Mwah…

Mwah… Anyway, we need to get these Gurls Bitchified. Has the College-of-Pimps arrived yet?

Yes, they have arrived. All one hundred and twenty of them. They'll assembly into the Holy Conclave of Pimps, be dressed in their inoculation robes and wait for us in the FUCIT Cathedrals Inoculation Chamber.

Have they been cleansed yet?

Yes, the Blessed Sisters of Pimps have performed the, Sacrament of Pimp Cock Cleansing. And all the Pimps have presented themselves to the PWN Gurls for servicing.

Good, everything is almost ready then.

Hours later....

Sister Tasty! (EN04) Have the chosen Sissies been prepared?

Yes, Cardinal Rimme. (The Sissy-Sister bows in reverence to the Cardinal). branded PWN Gurls of the Blessed Sisters of Pimps have performed the Sacrament of the Holy **Rosebud**® to the chosen ones.

Excellent! Did that go well?

Yes your Holiness, (Pimp Yaoi bows to the higher ranking Pimp Rimme when in the presents of others) their delicate flowering loveholes have been bloomed into beautiful Holy Rosebuds and are ready for the Inoculation Ritual.

Good, and lastly Sister **Tasty** have the new potential Whores been prepared for the Inoculation Ritual by performing the Sacrament of Holy Ointment?

Yes, the Pimped Whore Nuns have applied our Cock-Popes Holy Cream® by rubbing it into their Un-Inoculated Sissy cunts to lube and purify them of sins.

Good, their cunts have been cleansed with our Holy Cock-Popes Love-Cream® excellent!

In the mean time we can get prepared by cleansing and lubing each other for the ceremony in the ritual chambers vestibule. (Yaoi suggestively says while winking at Rimme).

Yes Pimp Yaoi. You have always prepared me well for an Inoculation. (Into the private vestibule they go).

A while later...

Okay, it's time to make these Sissies Whores® of the Holy Cockolic Church. Mwah…

Mwah… Yes, Cardinal Rimme. We will make them Pimped-Whore® Nuns tonight so they may faithfully serve the HCC.

Yes, Pimp Yaoi, though it is ironic, no one outside of the Church will ever know of their positions in the HCC. They will appear to be lazily floating along through life without a care in the world, attending school, doing their trivial US Federal civil servant Whore® jobs and breeding Sissies, while all the while faithfully devoting themselves secretly to serve the Church and promote Cockolicism.

Yes my adorable Holiness and all because they were the Chosen Sissies. Mwah…

Mwah… Yes Pimp Yaoi. Made into Rosebud-Gurls of the HCC, cleansed with the Holy Cream Ointment of our Cock-Pope® and will be inoculated with our Blessed Pimp-Cream® branded with the sign of a Pimped-Whore® and then seduced to serve and worship a Holy-Pimp for eternity. Huh! These are memorable times (Rimme sighs).

Oooh! And to also take their solemn vows of promiscuity, secrecy, and obedience, to be cum Pimped-Whore Nuns in a Harem and ultimately perform the duties of a Branded Whore Nun of the HCC.

Yes of course Yaoi. You left out the part about them being partially owned by us. It reminds me of something I learned in Seminary school. There're centuries of proof, once a Sissy has taken her vows and be cums a Pimped-Whore® Nun, she never leaves the HCC. And the PWN spends the rest of her life worshiping and giving praise her Pimps Holy Penis.

Yes Pimp Yaoi this is all true. For the grace of Cock our God and Savor, the PWN Gurls someday will assume one of the highest positions in all of Sissydom® the position of a Free Pimped-Whore®. They will take their solemn vows and receive the Sacrament of Holy Pimp-Cream® into their Sacred Sissy loveholes, now and forever. Amen.

[3.2] BACK

Two days later, back in the dorm Sunday afternoon...

Mary... (Still in a fog, Jane cums out of a two day long sedation and rolls over onto Mary to wake her up). Mare! Wake-up!

Ummm... Sleep... Jane. Get off of me!

Wake-up Honey! Mwah… Mwah…

Go to sleep Jane! Ummm... What time is it?

It's morning or no maybe afternoon. Wake-up Mary!

What? I need to sleeeeeeep Jane, I'm tired!

Mary, we were in Yaoi's office and now we're NOT!

Okay. Ummm... Jane for the Love-of-Cock, I'm sleeping go AWAY! (Mary curls up into the fetal position and pulls the comforter over her head).

Mary, I'm serious, get up!

Jane! You're serious? Huh! It must be a sixty-nine-alarm fire. Okay, WHAT? Ouch! I'm really tired! (Mary is finally roused and sits up).

I think something happened to us last night. Wow! My head. Oooogh!

Where did all these bouquets of flowers cum from? Did we go dating last night? Oooh my heads in a cloud! Ow! And my bottom. Ouch!

Ahhh... I'm actually a little dizzy too, Mare.

Okay think, what did we do last night? And why am I covered in this weird sperm goo... Hmmm... Sniff. (Mary takes a lick and sniff). Well, it tastes good! Hmm... Not bad. Kisss. Ooooh Jane my head hurts and my cunts really sore. I'm think we got into something we'll regret. Ahhh...

I don't know Mary! All I remember is seeing big ladies with gigantic horse-cocks. Huh! How bad can that be!

Ooooh, shoot! (Viscous goop cums flowing out of Mary's Vaganus). I have this cummy goopy stuff oozing out of my coochie like a river. Is your cunt sore too Baby? Uooogh!

Here let me taste it! (Jane gets between Mary's legs ready to go in for an exploratory cunt-munching).

[3.3] ROSEBUD

Okay! I'm going in!

Huh Jane! (Mary sighs). Do you always need to have sex? And just wait Baby, at least go wash your hands and arms with antiseptic soap before you fist me. Mwah...

Mwah... Oooh sure Mare! Sorry, we always follow sex-hygiene procedures. (Jane quickly washes up and moments later cums out of the bathroom with her arms up as if she scrubbed before surgery). Okay, I'm ready to go exploring! Heee hee...

Jane! Really? You wanna fist me and we can't figure-out what happened to us? Are you sore too? Maybe fisting isn't such a good idea Honey-Bun.

Cum-on Mare! You love when I'm elbow deep in your tunnel-of-love. Mwah... Ummm... Mwah... But yeah, I'm kinda sore too. Ow! It feels like I took a hardcore FO. Okay! I'll live!

Wow! Jane, you never stop wanting to have sex, even with a sore twat! Geeezzz... Take a break Sweetheart. Mwah...

Heee hee.... I'm going in, wish me luck! (Jane lifts up the hem of Mary's nightgown to discover a sexual treasure). Wow! HOLY POOP! Check out your Vaganus®. I was kidding about the tunnel thing! But Wow! Mary Congratulations, your cunt got bloomed too! (Jane is as excited as a Sissy kid on Cock-Mas morning). Un-fucking-believable!

OH POOP! I have a Rosebud? (Mary leans over for a better look). Ooooh Jizz-Us! (Mary reaches down and scoops out a palm full of the goopy substances from her now gabbing wide cavern of love).

Yeah isn't it cool? I love it Mary! You're like a Certified Whores now, **DSW** [2.B2.6].

Okay stop playing with it Jane! Only Doctorate PhD Sissy Whore (DSW) Gurls have Rosebuds. Ooooh! Honey! Jane STOP it! (Mary is obviously not in the mood). Take your arm out of my pussy! Geeez… Jane what am I going to tell my parents? They'll freak-out.

Well we'll just recite from our lecture notes. Tell them, you got, branded by a Pimp Lady, your cunt got bloomed into a Rosebud, you were ritualistically screwed by a beautiful FEM with a gigantic cunt probing appendage and you have no freaken clue how it happened!

THANKS! Sounds like a perfectly plausible story that, NOBODY is gonna believe. It does look pretty cool though, Hmmm…

You're right Mare, but there's one thing I do know. Mwah…

Mwah… What's that Jane?

I know something rimmed me and it was really BIG! Bigger than any Stud® dick I've ever had. More like a baseball bat, because my pussy still feels like something is stuff up inside it.

Mary inspects Jane…

Okay, well we both have sort bottoms. So this leads me to only one conclusion. Sit down here my cute little Bitch and spread your legs, it's time for your pussy examination! (Mary says jokingly as Jane plops down on the sofa. Mary then lifts up the babydoll Jane has on and goes in for a peek at her sweethearts pussy). Oooh my Cock-God, Jane! Cum on, we're going to the Hospital right now!

Why? Whatta!

Jane, your cunt bloomed into a Rosebud! You have a prolapsed hole! We have to go see a doctor! Someone hurt you! What-the-fuck! If I catch the asshole who hurt you I'll fucking orgasm him to death! Nobody hurts my Bitch!

Huh! Whoa, whoa, whoa... Mare! You gotta admit, I do have a beautiful rosebud. Oooooh! I can wiggle it!

But Jane we don't even know who did this!

Mary! I AM OK! I think it's wonderful! I have a Rosebud! Wow! Look how big it is, cool! I've always wanted my cunt to bloom! And it's permanent. Look, it wouldn't go back inside like it does after you fist me.

Honey, you've been violated and you need help, let's go, you need to have a doctor look at it right now!

Mary, STOP! I've always wanted to have a Rosebud. I've prolapsed every time you've fisted me. It's cool. There's nothing wrong with me, I just have a sore ass-cunt, but relax! I'm fine. There's nothing wrong about a Sissy cunt getting bloomed into a Rosebud. I'm proud I got bloomed. Look it's like I have big pussy lips! (Jane admires her cunt lips in the mirror).

Jane! Nobody messes with my Bitch! Nobody touches my Gurl!

Mary, yes I'm your Gurl, but I'm also a women now, don't you love me? Mwah…

Mwah… Of course I love you Jane, kiss…. (Hugs and kisses).

Mary, just calm down and take it easy, my cunt, our cunts are beautiful. They bloomed like red roses. And I'm fine, it doesn't hurt. Besides, when I've screwed gangs of Stud boys I wish I had a Rosebud. And you know me I get a little aggressive in bed so this is only going to let me enjoy sex even more.

Great! We mysteriously get our cunts surgically modified and you're just like, hey cool let's test them out! Okay, what's going on here Jane is my question? Someone obviously had a doctor perform a pussy blooming procedures, **PBP** [4.D-G1.1] on you and I and I wanna know who the hell gave them authorization to perform a major medical procedure on my Bitch! Dam-it! Where's my watch?

Relax boss. Mwah… Here it is.

Mwah… Thanks Honey.

Well Mary just calm down, I'm fine, you're fine. We're not bleeding or anything. It's cool! Mwah…

Mwah… Jane, why are there tan-lines on your ass?

Oooooh! What? I don't know!

Jane! Oh my COCK-GOD! It's freaken Sunday at four o'clock in the after-fucking-noon! Where the freak did 48 hours go?

I don't know Mary, but that's what I was trying to tell you when I woke you up. This is super weird. Maybe we were abducted by aliens and got probed. Uooooh…. Spooky!

Huh! It's not funny Jane! I'm gonna get a drink do you want something?

Yeah get me a bottle of strawberry **StudCream**®.

[3.4] BRANDS

The Gurls also discover the brands…

Wait! Mary, what's that on your ass? It's cute!

Where?

On your ass. Lift your nightgown up. Oooh! This is interest. Hmmm…

After what's been going on, don't play around Jane. What is it?

Wow! Don't tell me Miss conservative proper Sissy Lady got a tattoo on her ass? Hmmm… Yeah I knew you had a rebel in you. You got a Tattoo!

Tattoo! No freaking-way!

Wow Mary. Huh! This is a side of you I didn't know!

No I didn't get a freaken tattoo. (Mary looks at it in the mirror). Wait it's not a tattoo and it feels kinda sore. Ouch!

Wait, turn around Jane.

What for?

Just turn around. (Mary checks her lovers ass out). Yep! You got one too. It figures. We both went through the same identical processing.

What? Ouch! Don't touch it!

Oooh my Cock-God! It's not a tattoo it's a brand. Holy Sissy Crap! MARY! We've been branded!

You mean like the ones FEM ladies give their Pimped-Whores?

YES! Oooh holy Pooplactions! This might be the best thing that ever happened to us!

Jane, stop! What the hell is happening to us?

Mary! Huh! Who cares! Maybe we got Bitchified?

That's crazy Jane! And hey! We have really cool **Rosebud**® pussies but I'm scared!

Mary take it easy, the Professors told us the FEM ladies are a secret group of Sissies with enormous pricks.

Jane! And you believe that bullshit story? I mean serious, the FEM ladies resemble the United States government and they go around screwing innocent Sissies in the ass. Really? It's just fantasy, hokum, and nonsense! It's all

Bullshit... !!!...

These FEM creatures with enormous dicks are a figment of the Professors imagination!

But the Professor said....

Jane I could care less what they spew out in class. I don't think they really exist. It sounds like some made-up story, a myth people concocted, like a religion. People, especially Gurls, love a story about monster cocks. Are we in a dream? This is all really weird! (Mary has a soliloquy moment of rambling). Branded asses and a Rosebud®, I mean, Jizz-Us!

Cool! Check it out! (Jane, while passively listening to Mary's ranting, checks-out her newly decorated ass cheek). The brand is the **PWP**® symbol with a serial number, it means I've been (Jane looks at here ass cheeks in the full length minor) Pimped!

Jane! It's a fantasy. There's no such thing as FEMs and Pimps, Harems and...

Look at me! I'm a Pimped-Whore! Cool! (Jane zones out, humming and dances around Mary in a gleeful state of euphoria). I should get a lot of whistles by Stud dudes walking around with this on my ass? Hey I wonder who my Pimp is. But she's or he or whatever has got to be a FEM Sissy right? Well, whoever it is, now that she branded me, I'm that Pimps Bitch. God Mary! I'm a Pimped Bitch!

Sure you are Jane. Just keep prancing around in you Babydoll fantasizing about large penises. You little space cadet. I'll figure-out what really...

Mary! Aren't you proud of me? Look at my ass and Rosebud. I'm a Pimped Bitch!

Jane! I thought you were my Sissy-Bitch? Now you're someone else's Bitch?

No Mary, I'll always be your Promised® Bitch you know that, I'm Promised to you. I'm wearing your DOM collar and your engagement bow on my clit. This Pimped-Whore stuff, it's just sex business Mary. I'm not going to fall in love with some Pimp. I love you and I'll always love you. Kiss... Hmmm... Kisssss.

Wow! I have to admire it. My cunt got bloomed! I love looking at it in the mirror. Check it out Mary. (Jane wiggles her ass, pointing it at Mary to put on a show). Wow! Look, I can make my cunt open and close with my muscles! Look how wide it is. You can stick a beer bottle up my lovehole! Isn't it beautiful in full bloom? Do you like Mary? I feel so sexy, with my cunt wide open. I feel fantastic I'm a Pimped Sissy Women Now! I'm so proud Mary!

[3.5] PLOT

Mary theorizes about it being a plot...

It could be a government plot, a conspiracy.

Wow! Mary, just embrace our liberation. We should be celebrating our new pussy freedom! We could be dreaming of all the pleasurable possibilities.

Jane, I'm thinking we were just processed for use as advanced Sex-Slaves for the government. Our Rosebud® pussies are just a hybrid ATM for the USA Inc. bureaucrats to profit from.

Wow! Mary, please just enjoy what we have. And hey! We both know the government is always up to trying to bleed a few more bucks out of workers and Gurls like us, but who cares!

Huh1 (Mary sighs). Maybe you're right Jane.

[3.6] RITUAL

The Gurls analyze the chronological events…

Okay Mary, I hear what you're saying, but let's not get too excited and weirded-out. The important thing is we're together and we're not injured. Let's just calmly think about what happened, one moment at a time. Okay, so we went to class, lunch, and class then to the NSA meeting. Okay, I'm clear up to there.

Yeah me too Jane. Then we knocked on the door of Professor Yaoi's office. You were insecure, so I reassured you as usual. We went in, pleasantly said hello and sat down.

Right, then started talking and then they awarded us the NSA internship and scholarships.

Ah huh, then Yaoi asked if we wanted tea and… (The Gurls simultaneously shout), TEA!

We drank the FUCKING TEA! (Mary shouts).

And there was RimMe and Yaoi smirkishly smiling at us. They tricked us!

Yeah for sure! I remember trying to tell you I love you before I blacked out.

Jizz-Us, it was Yaoi and Rimme! Those conservative, mild mannered, Amazon ladies drugged us!

Wow! My cunt's really sore Jane. But like you said, it sure looks great, check-out the beautiful pinkish red color of my rose peddles.

It looks really beautiful Mary. Kisss... Kisss... Oooh Honey, don't you want me to lick and eat-out your Rosebud for you?

No Baby. Mwah... My cunt's too sore and it feels like there's still an enormous dick stuffed up my cooch. Like the dick never pulled out after doing me. I'm Okay. And I know we're going to do a lot of playing with our Rosebuds. But right now I'm just so confused and worried, I don't feel like playing. Like, where did all the time go?

The Gurls recalling memories...

Mare, all I know is, I remember these tall women, lots of women in long red robes and big enormous pricks sticking straight out of a big slit in the front of the robe. They were so long and thick and the beautiful women were proudly stroking their big dicks to full erection. Some were even stroking each other.

Yes, now I kinda remember that, but with less details. I do remember being on an altar or bench or whatever it was covered in red velvet and I was in a missionary position with my legs held apart by the red robed big **Dickgurl** ladies or whatever they were.

Yeah, yeah... Dickgurls.

It was warm and I was naked except for my six-inch pumps. And my whole body felt warm. I was covered in this warm sticky gooey stuff. It looked like cum but thicker. It must have been Man-Cum® because it smelt cummy and then I licked at the goo and thought it tasted great then I knew it was cum because nothing tastes better than cum. I felt hungry and started licking the thick cum off my body. Tell me what you remember Jane?

Okay, I remember being covered in gooey cum and licking it off myself. And yeah I was also in missionary position. There was this really tall woman in front of me with the biggest dick I've ever seen in my life. She was also wearing a red robe and on her robe there was the **Cock-and-Balls**

symbol of the Holy Cockolic Church across her large busty chest. She approached me with her threateningly large club of a prick and pointed the big appendage at my pussy and was teasing the entrance of my lovehole with it. I remember this explicitly because I was so crazy horny for her to shove it in my cunt. I was begging her to penetrate me.

Oooh! Jane, they tortured you. Ahhh... Mwah... My poor Baby. Mwah... (Mary hold Jane to comfort her).

Yeah! Then after her dick head penetrated my quavering Vaganus® she put her hands up over her head and was chanting some words which included my name and then when she stopped, the other robed women responded with some words just like they do at Cockolic Church during Sunday mass. Blah, blah, blah, the chosen one, Jane! Blah, blah, blah, the chosen one, Jane! On and on, again and again, go figure!

Ooooh! You poor Baby Mwah... (More parental hugs and kisses).

No Jane I'm blank on the religious stuff, but when I was on the Altar I looked over and saw you next to me and you were being plowed by what looked like a baseball bat sized prick. Only horses have big dicks like that, like the ones we had at summer camp! As thick as a soda can and super long. And like you, it was the biggest dick I've ever seen! And the woman doing you was beautiful. The front of her robe was open and I could see her big firm tits, I mean they were huge boobs! With big large nipples which were obviously lactating because her tits were squirting tit-milk all over the place as she screwed you.

And then Chanting and a pipe organ, I heard a pipe organ and a choir singing and it looked like a big Cathedral with a really tall vaulted ceiling. There were candles, lots of them. Lots of big candles and incense burning like the kind you smell at Cockolic Church that smells like Man-Cum.

And then the next thing I knew, it started raining sperm goo. The women were standing several feet away and jerking their huge appendages. Then they started spurting and shooting their dick-cream. Hurling long ropes of Jizzies through the air that landed all over me. I remember being hungry and opening my mouth to try and catch their love juice.

Wow! Then what happen Mare? (Jane is hinged on Mary's every word).

And then they came closer and started putting the tips of their dicks up to my lips. I felt dizzy the entire time. But their Jizz just kept shooting into my mouth and I remember having my mouth open as wide as I could and gagged on the amount I was trying to swallow. I kept going in and out of consciousness. It was one big blur.

Mary, I remember that part too with the Jizz spewing from the tall Amazon type women. And a women who looked a lot like Yaoi with a king size gigantic pole screwing me for I don't know how long. But oddly, I felt absolutely no pain. Mary you know I have an extra wide hole, but her tool was a telephone pole size dick. I just thought it was odd I wasn't screaming in pain from it.

Yeah Jane you're wide because you falsified your birth certificate lots of times to fool the doctors into thinking it was your time of the year, your birthday, for you to have your hole widening COWP®. And Jane it's why you have a lovehole wider than mine. I don't break the rules, Wildflower.

Ooooh Mary... kiss... kiss. I love being your Wildflower.

Anyway, on the flip side of that. Then I was surrounded by hot looking Sissies on a beach. They were a little older than us, with brands on their asses just like our brands and of course they were wearing the **Cock-n-Balls** Cockolic Church religious medal around their necks. They were licking, fisting, kissing and caressing me. All of them were extremely beautiful Sissies, with beautiful long hair and soft hands. They massaged me and I was being rubbed and probed by so many hands and tongues. It was like making-out with sixty-nine Sissy Babes. I was constantly squirting Jizz loads. It was like I was in paradise!

You were in paradise? Sissy Babes! And I wasn't there, Jane?

You were nowhere in sight Mare.

Okay! Now I really don't like what happen to us!

Mary? Cum-on. Don't be like that.

Jane! You know I get jealous.

Mary? Hey, (Jane puts her arms around her Lover and squeezes her tight and French kisses her ear and says). I love you Mary. (Jane says in a very soft and loving voice). I don't care what happen with some Sissy Babes, I love you and only you forever, sniff... kiss... Mwah…

I love you too Jane. Kiss... sniff... Kiss… You just scare me some times.

Huh! (Mary sighs). Yeah, the beach, I remember a beach too. Jane it was a beautiful white sandy beach, talk about paradise. There was a warm breeze and palm trees. Then I remember sipping on a cummy flavored Margareta!

Sounds wonderful to me. (Jane proclaims).

Explain that? Oooh, Poop! What the hell happen to us? I'm delusional. Slap me! And there were pretty super-model looking Sissies massaging me on a lounge at the water's edge, the sea water was washing over my feet and they were making out with me rubbing my tits, fisting me and sucking on my nipples and Cockette. Then I exploded into the Sissy who had my Cocklet and balls in her mouth! Talk about wet dreams.

Okay, Earth to Mary? Hello! You're Promised to me remember! Chicks on the beach! (Jane starts having a little pissy-fit about Mary cheating on her and jumps up to storm out of the room).

Jane! (Mary latches on to her lover). Calm down, there's no one else but you Honey! You know you're my only Bitch?

Do I Mary? Are you screwing around on me?

NO! Jane! NO! I would never cheat on you.

Are you looking for a new Bitch?

Jane! Stop it that will never happen. It was a dream! This whole thing was probably implanted in our minds by those two psycho Professors who drugged us.

Cummy-Margaritas and hot Sissies! Yeah, so I guess we know where we both got tan lines from? Mary you have tan lines like you had a Sissy bikini on and you always wear a one piece suit.

Jane I have no idea! But I never cheated on you and never will!

Sniff... sniff... Jane (Mary hugs Jane tightly).

Hey! I love you, you know I'm yours!

Sniff... (Jane, like Mary also has insecurity issues). Sniff... (Tears and more hugs).

I'll be your DOM forever. And if I had sex with another Sissy, I'm sorry! I was drugged by those crazy FEM ladies. Sniff... Sniff...

Yeah Mary and you were screwed by a FEM and FEMs are Sissies too. So what's it make me your Bitch on the side?

Jane relax it wasn't consensual sex! And Honey, I'm just as frightened by this stuff as you are. Let's just work it out like we usually do.

Sniff... yeah, yeah... I just don't want to lose you Mary! Sniff... Sniff...

Mwah... You won't Jane, I promise. Hey, providing any of this stuff is true, there's the rule we learned in class about PWP®.

Rule number 13, FEMs can't marry Sissies so don't worry about losing me. And there's the other rule they can't cum between Sissies. So let's just stop worrying about whom unknowingly cheated on whom. Baby Mwah… Hmmm... Kiss... I love you sweetheart.

Mwah… Love you too. (Jane says in a conciliatory voice).

Hey Jane. Look, I have NO idea what happen to us, but we obviously went from a Church kinda ritual where we were Rimmed-Out by Women with enormous pricks, probably Yaoi and Rim Me. We were bathed in man-goo and fondled by a gang of beautiful branded Sissy Babes on a beautiful beach. If you have an explanation, please share it with me?

Aliens! Mary we got PROBED!

Haaa... haa... haa ha... heeee... ha… (They both crack-up laughing about their predicament). Heeee… Hee…

Huh! Very funny Jane. Mwah… My sweet Honey-Bunny! You always have the funniest smart ass answers when we need one.

Mary, let's just account for the worst and the best of what happen.

Sure Jane! We'll sort it all out into Pros and Cons.

Okay, the worst stuff, the Cons.

(1) We were not in control of the things happen to us. (2) We were drugged. (3) Loss of time. (4) We might have had our Sissy Rights violated. (5) Medical procedure without our consent.

Okay, now the positive stuff, the Pros.

(1) Erotic experience with a hundred or more extremely large pricks. (2) had sexual intercourse by said, extremely large dicks. (3) Gallons of great tasting Jizz ejaculated into and or onto us. (4) Beautiful flowers delivered to our dorm. (5) Trip to a beautiful beach. (6) Branded with really cool prestigious Pimped Whore brands on our asses. (7) Licked, sucked, fisted, caressed, fondled, kissed, massaged and petted by beautiful branded Sissies Babes. (8) NSA internships and scholarships. (9) Our Sissy cunts magically bloomed into beautiful Rosebuds.

Yeah Mary! There's way, way more cool stuff about what happen then not. And we're probably the envy of every Sissy in the world! I mean we're Rosebudded, Pimped and Branded. So Babe, for a Sissy, it doesn't get any better than this. I agree with you Jane. Like I said, providing all this stuff about FEMs isn't bullshit, maybe I over-reacted.

Mare, a lot of cool stuff did happen to us.

Jane, do you like my Rosebud?

Cum here! I'm going to suck your Rosebud® all night. Ummm... Mwah... I love you!

Oooh Baby, I'll eat-out your Rosebud forever. Kisss... Ooooh! Fist me Baby! Lick me. Yeah! Stick your hand up my coochie, all the way up to your elbow Baby! Yeah! Yeah!

Hmm... (Jane is munching on Mary's juicy twat). Ummm... Tasty... Aaagh! God it's awesome your Sissy-Poop® tastes like sweet Man-Cream. Hmm... Gulp... I love it! Hmm..... Kisss... Kisss... (The sucking, fisting and making-out goes on for quite a while).

[3.7] MILLIONS

Many orgasms later…

Ooooh shoot! I forgot we have to order textbooks online for the Sex Education and World Domination classes.

Oooh, my favorite!

Huh! Yeah Jane! If it was up to you it would be your only class.

Mary why do you think I love you so much?

Tell me Jane I'm curious? I always wondered. Wait, is it because I'm beautiful and a great lover?

Well, yeah that too, but also because someone has to be in control around here and it ain't me!

This is true! For sure my Gurlfriend. I am definitely in charge.

Hey! Kisssss Thanks (Jane hugs Mary) for being there for me.

Ooooh! I love you Jane, sooo much. Okay, here's the FUCIT bookstore website. Oh! I'd better check my bank balance first. I'll enter my password and the balance is? Ahhhh… What the!

What?

Ooooh, I'm just surprise at my balance but after this weekend why should I bother thinking anything could be strange.

What's up?

Huh! Nothing. There was a million dollars deposited in my bank account yesterday. Huh! Unreal.

Cool! (Jane exclaims). This weekend just keeps getting better. Alright, hey check mine.

Okay, I just have to enter your password.

It's **marysbitch**.

Yeah I know your password Jane. It's always been **marysbitch**. Kisss... Hmmm... kisss... Hmmm.... And it's the same thing. One million was deposited yesterday at the same time, six-o-nine, to the second.

Cool! I wanna buy one of those Playboy Bunny outfits you like, the one with the big fluffy white bushy bunny tail butt plug and bunny ears. They're so cute!

Yeah, so where are you gonna go dressed up like a bunny Jane? Hmmm... Mwah... Babe, there's only one person who's going to see me dressed-up like a sexy party bunny. Only you Mary, only my DOM Babe can have me. I'm your Playboy Bunny Mary. Hmm.... Mwah... I want to make your Sissy Cocklette so freaken hard you start squirting Jizzies just by looking at me, Ummm... Mwah...

Mwah... I love you Jane! You're my horny little bunny. Hmmm.... Kiss... Hmmm.... Kisssss... Hey Jane, you can buy thousands of bunny outfits with a million dollars. The real question, and there are so many, is where in the world did the money cum from?

I know, add it to the growing list. But Mare, the money goes in the cool-stuff side of the list. The Pros. Mwah...

Mwah... Jane we have to meet up with the only people we know had something to do with this mystery.

Yaoi and RimMe! (The Gurls shout the same thing at the same time).

[3.8] PLAN

The Gurls hatch a plan to question the Professors...

Jane we need to go meet up with Yaoi or Rimme tomorrow and ask them all these questions about what's up?

Oooh! For sure! Mare we were obviously, from the little bits and pieces of vague memories we put together, part of some kind of a ritualistic ceremony.

Yeah! And it seemed it was centered on the two of us. We were both willingly engaged in sex with this religious type cult.

Right! Which by the way, appeared to be led by, tall, large breasted, beautiful Amazon women? Who all had, and here's the amazing part, the BIGGEST COCKS IN THE WORLD!

Amen to that Mary!

Hey my Vaganus® is sore but I ain't complaining! And hey I agree with yah Mary, let's go talk to Yaoi and Rim-Me tomorrow and ask them, how we can get more of this kind of action!

Oh Gurl! I'm still a bit skeptical about the validity of it all. But hey! I have some awesome memories and if they turn out to be true. Like you, I want more FEM action.

Sure, and here's a good question, now that we're branded and we assume we're, Pimped-Whores, who are our Pimps? Is it Yaoi and Rimme? Or are they going to auction us off to the highest bidding Pimp? I mean we're classified as livestock animals. Who knows what might happen.

Yeah Jane good point. But it's probably them. Okay, even accounting for the branded sore ass cheeks and our worn out loveholes that got bloomed, you have to admit. It was one hell of a goodtime weekend!

You know it Gurlfriend. I just wish the next time if there is a next time that we're fully conscious. Geeez… I'd seriously love to get boned again by the FEM ladies.

Me too Babe, but hey! Let's just relax, rest-up and study for class tomorrow and we'll figure it all out together? Mwah… Oh and Jane, I'm sorry I over reacted. And you know what part I like the most Jane?

What's that Boss?

It's the together part, being with you. Ooooh Babe! Cum here. Oh I love you so much! Mwah… Hmmm…. (hugs) kisss. We're together this is the only part that really matters. Mwah…

Chapter: 4 the Truth

[4.1] QUESTIONS

The Gurls go knocking for answers...

Knock, knock. (After last class the Gurls knock on the Professors office door).

Yes, cum in! (The door opens). Oh, Jane and Mary, we've been expecting you.

Hello Professor Yaoi, Professor RimMe. (The Gurls sheepishly enter).

Please close the door behind you. Hello Gurls, or maybe more appropriately, hello Ladies.

Professors, Jane and I have soooo many questions. And you and Prof Yaoi are the only ones we can link to the stuff that happened to us on the weekend.

Hmmm... Yes there were interesting yet necessary events which had to happen to you both this past weekend. And of course you have questions my dear Gurls. This is why we're here. We understand you both need answers and we will give them to you.

Yes, definitely Professor. The weekend was quite eventful, we went from nice sweet innocent Sissy-Gurls to Branded Pimped-Whores, our bottoms were bloomed into Rosebuds and oh yeah, a million dollars magically shows up in our bank accounts, supposedly we're Whores for Pimps we've never even met, because our asses got branded, and NO, we're not going to drink anymore of your

MAGIC-FUCKING-TEA...!!!...

Snifff... Snifff.... (The Gurls nervously shiver while holding each other for comfort).

There, there... Everything is okay my dears Gurls! Please trust us. Just calm down, we have answers. Please trust us.

Yes of course we trust you both. And I'm sorry Professor! Just please tell us what the hell is going on here? I mean, we're not mad at you or anything. Sure I was in shock and felt violated at first but then it dawned on us we weren't hurt or anything.

No, of course not. And you will never be harmed.

We just kinda wanna know what happen to us? Because it was done while we were in a semi-conscious state, so we're not here to cause trouble with you ladies or anything.

Just the opposite Professors, Mary and I wanna know when we can do it again.

Yes, Jane's right. We trust you but we just need to know the, who, how, when and where stuff.

Yes... Yes... my dear Mary, you're both confused I'm sure.

That's an understatement Professor!

Yes, we know you deserve answers and we have all the answers for you. Let me add here the answers will all be good news for both of you. Like I said, rest assured you Sissy-Gurls will never be harmed by us.

[4.2] FOLLOW

Now Gurls, I mean Ladies, please follow us.

Where are we going Professor?

Please Mary, one thing you can both be sure of, you will never regret anything we ask of you. Please this way (The Gurls reluctantly followed the Professors to the bookshelf in Professor Yaoi's office. Prof Rimme pulls one of the books, which happens to be the, Holy Cockolic Bible towards herself and the bookshelf quickly slides open).

Cool! This keeps getting better.

Yeah Jane the fascinating stuff never ends! Just hold my hand.

Please Ladies follow us. (They all pass through the wall and emerge into a hidden corridor).

Awesome a tunnel. (The Gurls follow the Professors down through the dark passages of the catacomb steps). COOL!

Jane, just hold my hand Gurl.

Minutes later...

Here we are, please step into the Chapel Gurls (It was a small enclave off the catacomb tunnel with large oak doors, and of course the Cock-n-Balls Cockolic Church symbol carved into them).

Okay Professors, why is there two compensation benches and an Altar in here?

Mary, this is our private Chapel where Professor Yaoi and I cum to hear Sissy Cum-fessions and to administer Penance. We also use it for recreational prayer and to give the Sacraments of Holy Cum-Union.

Prayer huh? Yeah I can see what kind of recreation we're talking about here and hey it's all fine and everything with Jane and I but Professors, it still isn't answering our questions.

Yes, of course, I just don't want to scare you young Sissy Ladies just yet.

Ahhh... Professor scary is when we woke-up, naked in nothing but our pumps on our feet, covered in man-goo with bloomed cunts and a branded ass, now that's scary!

Yes, undoubtedly it was, but necessary my Child.

[4.3] UNDRESSING

That's another thing Professor! You keep saying it was necessary, what exactly was necessary?

Yes, yes, as I promised you Mary. Now Professor Yaoi and I will make everything clear to you both. Professor may I?

Yes of course Cardinal Rimme, (Prof Yaoi turns with her back to Rimme and she unzips her dress zipper).

Now me. (Prof Rimme turns around with her back to Prof Yaoi and she unzipped her dress). Yes, my lovely friend I'd be glad to unzip you.

Ladies, we have something to show you, (The Professors are holding up their dresses with both hands over their chests) and we hope you like what you see. (The Professors glance at each other and with a nod simultaneously pull their hands away letting their dresses fall to the floor, around their ankles).

[4.4] REVEALED

Geeeeeeeeez! You can kill somebody with a dick that big. (The Gurls both stand there with their mouths wide open in total disbelief of the sheer size of the male appendages before them).

Ooooh my Holy Cock-God! Mary! It's soft yet still really long! Can you image it hard, Holy-Poop! I wanna get tortured with that thing! Wow! Huh! Their bodies are perfect.

Oh Jane, their so beautiful! These ladies must be FEMs! We were being taught about FEMs by FEMs and we didn't even know it! It's Unfucking believable!

[4.5] SCENE

Scene Description: The Pimps stood there still, posing before Jane & Mary so their perfectly shaped Amazon bodies could be admired. Both of them were beautiful beyond belief. They had large 48 DD breasts protruding firmly from their chests with large nipples dripping tit-milk. They had long flowing hair, beautiful eyes, all the female features of goddesses. Everything about them was feminine. Their hips and hour-glass contours of their bodies, they were female in every respect except for their large male organs.

To the Gurls astonishment both Yaoi and RimMe had what had to be the most magnificent specimens of the male sex organ imaginable. They were long to say the least, thick with large pulpous heads. They had the largest penises the Gurls had ever seen before in a fully conscious state.

Their long non-erect penises hung down to just above their knees and were strapped to the inside of their thighs. It was obvious, with their penises strapped down to their beautiful shapely legs, their long dresses covering their private parts, there was no mistake, the ladies were secretly hiding what they were most proud of for the sake modesty.

Ironically, despite having almost (The Pope has the longest) the world's largest penises, no one in the world above the catacombs concealed below the Sissyology building, would ever know of their secret lives as FEMs. Their true identities remain unknown with the exception now of the Gurls and a few sworn to secrecy members of the Cockolic Church, **HCC** [9].

[4.6] PWN

We know what you're thinking, and no my pretty little flowering Sissies, we've never hurt anyone with our blessed endowments. Nor has any member of the Holy College of Cardinal Pimps ever injured anyone. We believe we're here in this world to promote peace through penetration. And as I have stated, you Sissy Ladies will never be harmed.

You see Ladies, Professor Yaoi and I are obviously both, FEMCOCK® [8.1] Sissies and we'll never hurt either one of you. Huh! We're not humans! Remember the SDHS [15-69.4] rule,

Sissies do not hurt Sissies

Yes Professor, Sissies don't hurt Sissies.

Correct! And unbeknownst to the world, all FEM® Sissies are Ordained Pimps of the Holy Cockolic Church, the **HCC** [9]. We and the Conclave of Pimps have carefully chosen you Gurls long before you were ever born, to be our Pimped-Whore® Nuns, **PWN®** [9.2]. Over this past weekend you have both received the Sacrament of **Inoculation®** [8.3] and in doing so you were Bitchified® and made members of our Harems.

Shoot Mare, we are Harem Bitches!

We, your Pimps performed the Sacrament of Inoculation on you in the **FUCIT** Cathedral. And this would also explain the large sums of money deposited into your bank accounts at exactly the time of our orgasms inside of you. From that moment on, you both, not only were Bitchified but you also became our Whores. You were absolved of all of your worldly sins and your spirits and **Sex-Souls** [21.B.24.2] were both filled with the presence of the Holy Cock-Spirit.

But, Pimps, Professors, FEMs, hell, whatever you ladies are, we've been training all of our lives to be cum professional Whores in the new **MSES®** [4.D-G2.1] We want to be proud productive members of our society working as United States Federal Civil Servants. As Whores in the new morally liberated America. And now you're talking about making us Church Whores too. So, how many Whore® jobs can a Sissy have?

This is a good question Mary. You can be both actually. One Whore® position is as a civilian Whore in the world you're familiar with. The one you grew-up in. The one you trust and believe in. The wholesome productive Stud-Sissy Society of the United States Inc. what you know as the MSES!

But now, both of you are also in a, Pimp Whore Partnership, a **PWP®** [8.3] with us, your registered civilian Pimps. In your civilian Whore positions, you are Federal Civil Servants and are officially under our guidance according to the federal rules and regulations of the PWP® which are specified in the **MSES** documents. The guidelines are explained in the Sissydom Manual SM069. We don't make this stuff up. Section 8, Appendix H, Part A (1-7) and Part B (8-14).

The other Whore® position is a secret religious one as a Pimped-Whore of the HCC. You're now both in a secret religious Whore position as well as a Federal Civil Servant one. And no one must ever know about the positions you have in the HCC. Not your friends, family, the Priests back in your home-town parish who are hearing your mother's cum-fessions and especially not the Government of the Unites States of America Inc.

Whoa! This must be a dream or something!

No dream, as I said, all will be revealed to you. And I want you both to know, we have very careful decided to make you our Pimped-Whores. Based on all of the things we've learned about you. We didn't choose you only because you're both beautiful and talented Sissies. No, the selection process is much more complex than just having a fuckable ass-puss. The deciding factors were many. For example, Jane's Cockage®, Mary your intelligence, also both of your mothers are Whores for the Cockolic Church. And most importantly, both your families have ancestral history with breeding **FEMCOCK** [8.H1.1] Gurls.

WHAT? Get out of here! No way! No way is this possible!

Yes way. Sister Jane, both yours and Mary's families have bred a FEMCOCK Gurls at six point nine times in your family's cock-lineage.

Oh for the love of the Cock-God!

Yes, several hundred years ago there were FEMCOCK ladies in both of your families. There's no doubt about the DNA, your families cock-lineage records are archived in the Holy-Cock city, in the Vaticum in Rome and are sealed records because of your FEM history. We know things about you that you might not be aware of yourselves. The HCC has existed longer than any government or religion so we know everyone's cock history going back thousands of years.

Holy Sissy-Poop Jane...!!!...

[4.7] PATH

The Gurls need to decide their path...

Yes Gurls, Holy-Poop in deed. You are the chosen Holy ones to continue the FEMCOCK® lineage. Now for the details, Pimp Yaoi and I, as you may have already surmised, are devout members of the HCC and as our Harm Whores you will be expected to take your sacred vows as Nuns in the HCC and as Nuns you will serve our Cock-God® faithfully as we and also your mothers have done. So Gurls, this is the final point of no return. You'll be deciding your path. Are you both willing and ready to be cum Nuns and take your vows?

YES, YES, anything you want from us, Jane say yes Sweetheart!

Yes, yes, I want to belong to you too, I love your massiveness! I'll do anything for it! Me too! (Both Gurls are all-in).

Well, I see the Inoculation® is working. There will be much for you Pimped-Whore Nuns, PWN® Sisters to learn and practice as our Whores of the Church. As a branded Bitch of your Ordained Pimp you will be expected to mount and ride your Pimps Holy appendage in prayer when we cum-mand you to and when doing your penance. Or while receiving the Holy Pimp-Cream® potion in your blessed Rosebuds. And willingly dismount the Holy-Pimp when you are told to without whining or whimpering in wanton desire. You will also be expected every Sunday to attend mass with your Pimps and all the member of your Harem.

When here in the FUCIT Cathedral, you will be expected to wear your Nun garments and veils. Also you must confess your sins to your Pimp and as your mothers have done, you too will also do your penance by offering your sinful yet beautiful bodies to your Pimps.

Now Sister Jane go to your Holy-Pimp Yaoi, (Jane's mouth falls open in disbelief). Sister Mary cum to me my child. Mary please kneel on this billow before me and Jane please do the same in front of Pimp Yaoi. Now please un-strap our Ordained Holy-Cocks (The Gurls do as they are told, undoing the straps holding their Pimps long, soft limp shaft to the inside of their long, stocking clad legs).

Geeez… Mary it's the longest prick in the world!

Just do what you're told Jane!

Our blessed children of the Church take your Holy-Pimp in your hands and kiss the blessed tip of it in reverence of its magnificence. These are the Holy-Cocks which will be guided inside of you and be there for you to enjoy for the rest of your lives. Now let's bow our heads and begin the Holy **PWN Vows** [9.I5.2].

[4.8] PWN VOWS

The Gurls take their PWN vows of promiscuity…

Ooooh Holy Cock-God® in heaven, we place our hands on the heads of Sisters, Jane and Mary today to guide them to accept our Blessed Pimp-Cream® into their willing and deservingly so Blessed Sissy mouths so we may share with them the glorious Cream of your Cock our God. Amen.

Here before us today are Sisters, Jane and Mary, they have been well cumed into the Holy Cockolic Church [9], they have both received the Holy Sacrament of **Inoculation** [9.H1] with your Sacred-Cream® so that they may serve you our Holy Cock-God® forever. Now they will take their **PWN**® Vows [9.I5.2].

Do you Jane vow to obey and worship your Ordained Pimp forever and to live a life of servitude in the Holy Order of the Blessed Sisters of Pimps?

Yes Jane, say yes.

Yes I do. Amen.

And do you Mary vow to obey and worship your Ordained Pimp forever and to live a life of servitude in the Holy Order of the Blessed Sisters of Pimps?

Yes I do.

Amen. We shall now pray and share **Holy-Cream**® [9.I3.8].

[4.9] HBJ

The Holy Blow-Job (HBJ)...

Now let us pray the Holy **Blow-Job** prayer [9.I5.3]. For our sakes and the sakes of all the faithful our Holy Cock-Pope was blessed with the largest FEM Cock in Heaven and on Earth.

She offered up in erect form her Holy-Cock® and had her balls drained for us.

And Her Holy FEM-Cock® rose again after the third load in accordance with the Holy-Cock Scriptures.

Her Holy-Cock ascended into the Blessed Virgin Sissy Breeding vagina and has inoculated the Human Sissy Breeder for the Cock Father.

I believe in the Cock-God®, the Father almighty, creator of heaven and earth. I believe in the Sissy of the Cock-God, Gods only Daughter Jizz-Us® and our Savor. Under the American Government she was crucified, died and was buried. She descended into poverty after three bankruptcies and her penis rose again. She ascended into the bank heaven of consumer debt. I believe in the forgiveness of debt jubilee against Sissies. Our Lordess Sissy will cum again in glory to judge the living and the not feeling so good, Sinful Non-Stud working class in Sissydom® and Her Holy Cockolic Church will have no end. Amen.

[4.10] CUM-UNION

The Cardinals dispense their Cum-Union…

Gak… Guk… Uuuuh! Aaaagh! Swallow my **Holy-Cream**® [9.I3.8] my sweet blessed Whore Nun! Aaagh! Gulp... Swallow this Holy **Cum-Union**® [9.HS.2] my child so you may be saved! (Yaoi and Rimme both ejaculate copious amounts of cream into the Gurls mouths). Guk… Glrck…

Oh! Jane! It's too much Jizzie cream! Gak, Guk, Gulp! Glrck…

Keep swallowing like I showed you Mary! Don't stop! (Jane the blow-job queen shouts).

Ah! Aah! Aaagh! Nagh! Aaaagh! Oooooh! Sisters Jane and Mary, you may swallow. (The Gurls try desperately to swallow every drop of the voluminous amount of dick-milk pumped down their throats). Swallow our Holy-Cream® and be blessed with the Holy Cock-Spirit forever. Amen!

Kiss.... kiss... Mwah... I love you Mary and my Pimps prick (Unable to stop their adornment of their Pimps gigantic shafts both Gurls continue to stroke and stare in wonderment while they snowball with each other). Mwah...

I love you too Jane! I can't believe how beautiful their fucksticks are! There's soooo much cum! Oh! I got some up my nose! Kiss... Gulp... Slurp... Kiss. I'm in love with their dicks.

Spit the goo onto my face Mary! I wanna bath in Pimp-Cream! Creamy goo! Ahhh.... Spit.... Spit... Swallow it. Gulp... Kissss.

Me too! Jane, their love-bones so beautiful. There magnificent I don't want to let go of it! Slurp... Slurp... (Mary licks at the still erect tool). I gotta have it forever! Ooooh! Jane, I can't stop kissing and licking it! I want it inside of me!

[4.11] TURNED

Turning Mary the conservative...

Sister Jane, Sister Mary. I know you still have many questions.

Oh Professor! I have so many questions. But I don't care anymore your Holiness. I just want to serve you forever! (Mary is still hanging onto and kissing her Pimps erection). Mwah... Mwah...

Well, I understand you're in love with my penis and yes it is wonderful (Rimme gently rubs her cockhead along the side of Mary's face and taps her cheek with it). It will give you many years of pleasure. But my dear child, do you have any doubts?

Okay Pimp Rim Me, your right, I'm still a little fuzzy about the whole Church thing here. Professor I mean Holy Lady, whatever, huh! I don't know what I mean. I'm so crazy for your Cock! Mwah... Mwah... (She continues to worship what she idolizes).

Yes Sister, Pimp Yaoi and I are here to provide peace and comfort to you so please ask us anything you want.

Well okay, you call us Sisters and you guys are Holy Pimps?

Yes Mary, let me explain, but please continue to worship me with your mouth while I do so.

Gak.... Kiss... Hmmm... Gladly Professor, I'll always worship your Holy penis. I'll do anything you ask of me, just so I can have more of you inside me my Lord! Mwah... Gak... Guk...

Yes, you beautiful Sissy. You see Mary, Yaoi and I own you, so of course you and Jane will do everything we ask of you. And you may address me as Lordess or your Holiness.

Mwah... Yes anything my Holiness, please bang me with your magnificence! It's so enormous my Lordess! I need it! I need it up inside my vaganus! Oooh! Aaagh! Mwah... Guk, Gak... Slurp...

Oh my! Sister Mary! I can see you're so overwhelmed by my magnificence you've put your hand up your Rosebud and you're fisting yourself. My, my, you have a very strong desire my dear. Well, Sister Mary, every Sunday your Rosebud is going to be thoroughly attended to and filled with Holy-Cream®. And I assure you, you will be satisfied.

I will serve you my Lordess. Mwah… Guk, Gak…

Mary I'm relieved to see how the inoculation has totally Bitchified® you. I had some doubts because of your conservative DOM type nature that it would take longer to indoctrinate you into be cuming a faithful FEM worshiping Whore. But I can see now all this is of no concern to me anymore. Because Mary it's obvious I own you completely with the power of my Holy-Cock.

Oh! Without a doubt your Holiness! You own me my Lordess! Mwah… Gek, Guk, Gak… (Mary desperately tries to snake the entire length of the Cardinals shaft down her throat). Glrck…

Oh my! Now I know you're attracted to my Pimp-Cock Mary and this is all very natural. But first you and Jane must have special Pimped-Whore Nun training and the Sisters in your Harem will teach you how to service a Pimp properly. For example, as Sisters of the HCC you are expected to hold, lick, kiss, suck and fondle the penis and nut-sacks of your Holy-Pimp while she is in your presence. Basically, one of the many tasks you Nuns have to do is to constantly worship our huge Holy appendages.

It's just what Whore Nuns do, something you'll just have to do regardless of if you understand the religious protocol or not.

Okay Jane! Did you hear that? Are you good with this Baby?

Huh! Yeah are you kidding? Mary, I mean you don't have to ask me twice if I want this huge thing in my holes or not. Just look at the beauty of this massive prick! Mary it's the most precious thing in the whole world besides you Babe! (Jane never let go of Yaoi's erection and was still intoxicated by the taste and smell of it, licking and kissing it with abandonment).

Okay then! Sisters Mary and Jane, now that you have both taken your vows as Whore Nuns of the HCC there're things you need to know. Sisters, when we're in private, in the Church, like now, you may address us as, your Holiness, Lordess Pimp, Master, but never as Professor. Also, out of reverence of our positions in the Church when you arrive or depart our presence, you are to genuflect before us and kiss the tips of our Ordained Holy probing organs, while chanting your vows to worship your Pimp.

Yeah! Yes! My Holiness. I'll, I mean, we'll do anything you ask of us. (The Gurls still covered from head to toe with Jizzie goop shout their affirmation of devotion to their new owners while kissing the dickheads).

This is good! Kissing your Pimps boner is something you will both need to get used to doing.

Oh gladly! It's so beautiful my Lordess. I have never seen a more impressive penis in my life. Mwah...

Yes, this is right Sister Mary they are beautiful. (Yaoi and Rimme put on a show for the Gurls and rub their still erect cocks together which stimulates an ejaculation out Jizzzie streams onto the Gurls faces). Oh! And you will also need to receive facials. Ahhh... Ahhh...

Thank you for the facials my Lordess Yaoi and Rimme. Slurp... Slurp... (The Gurls massage the cream into their cheeks while licking the holy goop off one another). Slurp… Ummm… Yummy! Oh! It's so thick and delicious! Slurp…

Yes, yes… Anoint yourselves with our Holy-Cream. Rub it into your faces. And as much as we'd like to continue teasing you sweet Gurls, there is one additional thing I need to stress to you.

Yes my Lordess. (Mary says and the Gurls respectfully stop licking and assume a kneeling, subjugated pose on the floor in front of their new owners who towering over them).

Very obedient, good Gurls. So, religiously speaking, the HCC is very interested in using you both to its advantage. As do both Pimp Yaoi and I, we too profit and feel you are very precious, and you both will enjoy a profitable and glorious future in the Church for many, many years to come.

But your Holiness, me and Jane, we're just Gurls and we...

Mary my dear child. (Rimme interrupts her). Let me please.

Yes, I'm sorry I spoke my Lordess.

[4.12] FAITH TEST

Well, I want you and Sister Jane to take the **test** we spoke to you about.

What kind of test Pimp Rim Me? And what if we fail?

Failure is not an option! Sisters, this is a test-of-faith to your Pimp and to the **HCC** [9]. If you fail, you'll just need to submit yourselves to more behavioral training. So! It's a secret assignment, you'll be instructed what to do.

Anything for you my Holiness! You are my new owner and Master! (Mary says while looking down at her owner's feet).

Also Sisters **Mary** and **Jane**, you are to never speak of anything you have seen or heard while in the service of the HCC. We know you both have very strong feelings about the Sissy World. And it was partly why, because of these firm beliefs in Sissydom®, you were chosen to be Whoring Sisters of the Church.

Now I want to share something very important with you. And this is unknown by your typical Church parishioner. You see Gurls. The Holy Cockolic Church is what started Sissydom®. The HCC and Sissydom was founded by Sissies for Sissies.

Despite all the propaganda the USA Inc. government generates in Hollywood through the **HPC** [21.B.17]. The Church controls all branches of the new United States government. This is right down from your President Donald (the douche-bag) all the way to the lowly common Sissy Hoe licking the balls of all the Cunt-gressmen. Our members are in total control as was the Corporatocracy who destroyed the American economy hundreds of years ago.

The only real difference being is, when the Federal Reserve Bank, the **FED**® [4.D-G4.17] took over ownership of the US government it made everyone a debt slave in effect it financially screwed the entire US population in the ass also called Financial-Sodomy. And now, because of the Holy Cockolic Churches (HCC) intervention, just the opposite is happening. The benevolent HCC breeds you darling little Sissy sex-slaves and people screw them in the ass aka Vaganus®. So humans actually gain monetarily through workers labor compensation transaction, **LCT**®, of which the Church makes six point nine percent on.

This financial war has been fought for millenniums. It's a war between the **Money-Whore** [22.14.1] bankers and **Cock-Whore** [22.14.2] Sissies Like I said it's really quite simple, one takes money from you as they fuck you in the ass, the other one gives money to you when you fuck them in the ass.

Wow! Okay, I don't know what you're speaking about my Lordess. Perhaps penetration is necessary for a better understanding? (Mary is seriously trying to get laid).

Yes, yes, you impatient child. Mary, I will teach you many things impaled on me. But suffice it to say, this is the new America we're speaking about. You see Gurls, thanks to the well placed Cockolic Church politicians they did the same thing the bankers did to the US government back in 1913 with the Federal Reserve Act. This time the HCC secretly bought our Cunt-trie back from the **Money-Whores**.

Huh! The Church bought America? (Mary says with surprise in her face).

Yes Mary. Accept the legislation was called the United States Sissification® Act. Then the old FED was converted into the Financial Enslavement Deprivation [4.D-G4.17]. And the same as the FED, the Cockolic Church Bank by shear, strong-arm tactics, financially manipulated the desperate United States Inc. government into be cuming its central bank dominated Money-Whore again. And this is how the HCC bank purchased this America for pennies on the dollar without anyone knowing about.

So Americans nowadays go about living their merry lives of servitude by happily screwing Cock-Whores in the ass-pussy. But all the while they unknowingly are being financially controlled as serfs by the Holy Cockolic-Church Bank.

Huh! Holy-Poop. Us Sissies are like ATM machines for the Church!

Yes, yes… This is why the future of Sissydom® lies in the strength of the HCC. Through your devotion as Cock-Whores of the Church you strengthen the Church and all of Sissydom®.

Jizz-Us® Holy-Poop. Huh!

Yes, mountains of Holy-Poop my dear.

[4.13] WARNING

Okay lastly Gurls, if you obey your Pimps then you will live your lives unharmed, without a need for worry, with abundance and love. Or and I warn you both now, if you don't obey and break your sacred vows of secrecy and promiscuity you will both live a life of strife and hardship. Lives void of joy and be cum slaves at a C-Type Whoring-Station where you will work as a common Hoe for the rest of your lives, without praise, no dental plan, no Studbucks coffee, crappy cafeteria food or any meaningful benefit at all. So, do you want to take the test?

YES! YES! YES! We want the test my Lordess Pimp. YES, please my Lordess, I beg you to test us!

Ok my dear children. So, you'll go back to your cozy dorm and someday you will receive a special envelope. Open the envelope and follow the instructions. Everything you need will be provided to you to accomplish your test assignment.

Yes my Lordess Pimp. Anything for you! Kiss… (The Gurls kiss the dickheads of their Pimps). I worship your penis my Holiness. Oooh... Kissss….

Mwah… Oh course you do my dear, who wouldn't.

But my Lordess, will Jane and I, will we be together for the test?

Hmmm… (Pimp Rimme smiles). I knew you would ask this Sister Whore Mary. Yes, my child, in fact you and Jane will always be together. Now and in the future regardless of what is asked of you by the Church. You will never be separated from her. This is the will of the Church. Your union with your Bitch has been sanctified to last forever.

But my Lordess, Jane and I still have questions.

Yes, Sister Mary, I know you do my child and all will be answered in goodtime. Now is a time to put your faith in the Church and pray for the strength your Sissy pussies will need to serve your Pimps wishes.

Yes, your Holiness Rimme. We'll obey your wishes always. Mwah… (Mary, half her Mistresses height, looks up and says while blowing an air-kiss with her lips up at Rimme). Always and forever!

Mwah… Yes, you will my Dear. You… will… (Rimme squints her eyes and says in a Yoda type voice).

[4.14] DISMISSED

Now leave here the way we came, up the stairs through the catacomb. And Mary, everything that has happened and everything that will happen has a purpose for you and Jane, so remember this when your faith is tested and your pussies are sore.

Yes, my Lordess and Mistress. We will not lose faith.

Good! Now you may kiss our Holy probes good bye.

My Lordess? (Jane sheepishly asks).

Yes Sister Jane?

When will we have the privilege of having penance performed in our pussies like our mommies do with their Priests?

Haaaa... haaa… haa…. Oh my dear sweet Jane! Every Sunday during mass here at the FUCIT Cathedral, your pretty Rosebud® will be thoroughly probed and made pure again, I assure you.

Thank you my Lordess. Kiss... Kiss. (Jane has to prop herself up on her tippy toes just to give a kiss to the head of her Pimps still erect cock).

Goodbye my Lordess Pimp Rim Me! Kiss… (The Gurls kiss their Masters on the tips of their Holy pricks in reverence and genuflect as they say goodbye) Goodbye Pimp Yaoi.

Goodbye Pimp Rim Me. Mwah… (Mary blows air-kisses with her lips).

Oh! And Mary, when you need to cum to Church do you remember which is the secret book you pull to open the bookshelf?

Yes Pimp Rim Me. The Holy Cockolic Bible.

Good Gurl. Mwah…

Goodbye your Holiness.

Let go really fast Jane. (The Gurls go through the bookshelf and scamper across the FUCIT campus stile covered in Jizzie goop). I just wanna get home and shower off all this gelatinous goopy stuff the Pimps shot onto us. It's so thick!

Mare? Mary?

Yeah Jane. What's wrong Honey?

Don't let go of my hand. Pleeeease…

Jane! It's okay. Why are you squeezing my hand so tight? We're going to be alright. We're halfway home to our dorm. When we get there we'll talk about our Pimps and everything that happened to us.

Okay Mary, what I meant is, don't let go of me, (Jane stops Mary) I mean, sniff… sniff… don't lose me Mary. (Jane looks up into Mary's eyes with tears in hers).

Oh Jane! I'm not ever letting go of you sweetheart. Now cum on, let's stop worrying and hurry home. I'm gonna make us both a nice hot cummy-coco and then we can crawl into bed and hold each other tight all night, kisss… I love you. Mwah…

[4.15] DORM

Back home in the dorm…

Aaah… We're nice and cozy now. Ooooh hold me Jane. Honey, I went online and posted that our Whorehouse is closed tonight because of illness. The Stud boys don't have to know our cunts are still sore from the spectacular weekend we had.

Mary? Mwah…

Mwah… What Jane? What's wrong? You have a sad somber look on your face).

Are we really Nuns? Did we take the vows to be Nuns like our Mom's did?

Yes, yes… We're Nun like our moms.

Do we have to go to Church on Sundays?

Yeah, yeah… Jane you heard Pimp Rimme, our Pimps are going to help us with our new ad-DICK-tion. Hee... heee... During and after mass.

And don't worry about the Nun stuff I don't think our Order of Nuns does a whole lot of praying and when we do we'll be doing a Cow-Gurl on our Pimps pole while we're chanting it.

Haa haaa… Sounds good! Mwah…

Mwah… yeah, we're in the kind of Nun sect that gets our cunts stuffed and are flagellated with monster cunt probing fucksticks. So we'll be reciting nothing but HAPPY prayers of ecstasy! Haa... haaa... hee...

Oh! Cool! Then it's the best religion ever! Hey we've been going to HCC all our lives. I'm going to love being a Pimped-Whore Nun, Sister Mary. Amen!

Amen! Jane. But let's just see what happens. Those two Pimp ladies are secretive and I'm not sure they told us all their plans for us.

Oooh cum on! Tell me you didn't fall in love with the largest pricks we have ever, sucked, fondled, drooled-on, stroked or milked in our lives?

Yeah, yeah… Okay, I admit it, I love their big dicks! They're so big I'm in-heat for them. But not more than I love you Babe, kisss. I'm just still wondering if it was a dream. I mean, Dam Jane! They were so beautiful. I can't wait for Sunday.

Okay Mare than you are turned-on Miss Conservative?

Yes of course! What girl wouldn't be? It's just I don't want us getting hurt.

Mary you're doing the parental thing again. I mean, I get your apprehension, but this could be the best thing to ever happen to us besides falling in love with each other. Mwah…

Well my dear Jane, I'll go along with the whole cock worshipping thing, how could I not. And getting our cunts stuffed with the biggest pricks in the world, sure! Count me in. But you know me I'm gonna be a little cautious for the both of our sakes. There's school work, and...

Yes Mommy. (Jane says rolling her eyes).

Jane! You know I'm the one who does the worrying around here.

Yep! Mary, what would I do without you? Mwah…

Mwah… Ummm… Jane, I wouldn't do anything to jeopardize our relationship and I definitely always think of what's best for the both of us Sweetheart.

Yes, Mother-Superior.

Oh Jane. Cum here! Kiss... (Hugs) Mwah… Let's just get some sleep and dream about FEMs. Hmmm… Kissss. Oh Mary stick it in let's spoon. Hmmm.... Kiss… Mwah…

[4.16] THE ENVELOPE

Six days and nine hours later...

Mary, some express mail service dude just dropped this big package off marked, For Jane & Mary.

Oh! Freak it's here! (Mary jumps up in anticipation).

What? What's here?

The assignment!

Oh! The Assignment!

Yeah right, the test of faith.

Do you really think they're going to test our faith in the Church? Mary, I mean we're the hottest Sissy Babes on campus now. They ain't gonna excommunicate holy Sissy Babe's like us.

Yeah Sugar-Puss it's hard to believe we're both Nuns now.

Mary we're the only Branded, Rosebudded, Pimped-Whores at FUCIT! It's why there're boys banging on our door and a load of money in our bank accounts! We're hot pussies!

Well yeah! All fine and dandy my Lover Gurl but Jane, you being Euphoric about it could be dangerous. I really don't think the Pimps were kidding about our lives being ruined if we don't play ball with them. Take this serious Jane, it's no joke.

Okay Mother-Superior! Huh, let's see what our assignment is.

Here, plug-in the USB flash drive and play the message.

The Assignment...

Good Morning Gurls, your mission, Gurls, should you decide to accept it, is to,

Infiltrate the U.S. Gold Bullion Suppository in Fort Knox **Kuntfucky**, the new Kentucky. There you will prostitute yourselves to the hundreds of vault guards. The vault they guard is a highly fortified and protected area. With one of the most sophisticated electronic security systems in the world.

First an hour prior to being gang-raped by the entire guard staff, insert a sedative suppository up your Sissy loveholes. The sedative will have no effect on you because you're both mutated purebred **BfB** Sissies. The sedative will take effect, only on the human Non-Stud NS men, immediately upon their penetration of your beautiful **Rosebud**® pussies.

So upon arrival you Sissy-Gurls, dressed in the appropriate **FuckMe**® outfits, are to allure the soldiers guarding the front entrance by displaying your blossoming Rosebuds and then render them inoperable with your charms and tranquilizing Sissy pussies.

Afterwards disarm the security system by pressing the little red button on the special insecurity disabling device which came in the envelope. This will give the gold removal team the opportunity to empty the vault of its gold, if there is any and ship it to the Vaticum City in Rome.

Next, to finish your mission, go to the insecurity office where you'll find hundreds of horny, slacking-off security guards who will probably just be sitting around jacking off and jizzing onto the pages of Hentai comic books. There you will offer your Rosebuds to all of the hundreds of perverted Non-Stud (NS) soldiers. Continue to seduce and be penetrated as many times as is necessary to accomplish total sedation of all the NS guards.

Finally when you receive the signal that the gold has been safely removed, walk proudly straight out the front door with your now cum drenched dripping Rosebuds. There'll be a van waiting there for your safe get-away. The van is equipped with a portable Douche-O-Matic® for you to clean out your loveholes which were contaminated with icky Non-Stud Jizzies.

As always, should you or any of our Whore-Forces be caught or Fucked-Out (FO), our Holy Cock-Pope in Rome will disavow any knowledge of you being Nuns of the HCC. This flash drive will self-destruct in six point nine seconds. Good luck Gurls.

Three, two, one, Pissss... Pissss.... PUFF!

Huh! Whatta! The flash drive just melted! Dam! These guys don't screw around with the secrecy stuff.

Okay, so what's so hard about that?

Huh! Are you freaken kidding Jane! The guards have sexually lethal fucking GUNS! We can DIE from orgasmic seizure Jane!

No! We go, we fuck, we leave! What's so hard about that? The only guns the guards are going to whip out in front of us hot Sissy Babes are their little toy peanut size Non-Stud dicks.

Hey, here's info about the limo and private jet taking us to **Kuntfucky**. WOW! First class all the way! Oh and an unlimited gift certificate to the SissyWear® shop. Here's the security disabling thingy. And a box marked, SEDATIVES. Cool! Mary let's go shopping! I want to get some sexy Sissy cloths for the trip.

Hang on Wildflower. Or Hmmm… Should I call you wild rose bud? Jane, you've always been a wild little nympho Sissy ever since we were kids. You'd always want to go on another boy finding adventure. So to you it doesn't matter how dangerous the mission is. You'll always want to go in search of your next gangbang experience!

Mary! Stop worrying, God-of-Cocks! So all we have to do is, (1) go into this fort seduce the guards at the front door, (2) press the little red button then (3) screw with everyone in sight. Walla!

What's so hard about it? Easy peasy! We're mutant Sissy Whore animals breed in a test tube! We've been gangbanging since we were little kids. And hey, our government made sure we would have the sexual ability to do stuff like this.

Sure! Okay Jane and if we're caught, we go to a Non-Stud (NS) male forced labor prison and are common Hoes for the rest of our lives. And Honey, they don't even have manicurists, pedicurists or hair salons in NS prisons. How am I supposed to live like that? But sure no problem! Let's just go do something dangerous! I don't need a pedicure or my hair done. I'll just slum it.

Hey! I'm not fancy like you. Besides, it'll be fun Mare! Cum-on!

JANE! We have a good life here at school, like you said we're the hottest Sissies at FUCIT! There's money in the bank, I was just voted in as our new class president and we're the most sought after Sissy Gurls on campus. We can never screw the multitudes of Stud boys who cum to our Whorehouse. And on top of that we have this amazing, secret thing happening with a couple of the world's largest penises. Life is good Jane. Dam it! I just don't wanna lose this! (Mary goes into this insecurity rant, while Jane yawns).

Well, actually our Holy **Cock-Pope**® [9.I3.7], the main boss in Rome, has the largest penis in the world!

JANE! I'm not kidding.

Yeah, yeah… Okay Mary, I know you do all the worrying, but sometimes you just have to go with your cunt feelings about stuff. And right now I have a real tingly feeling in my pussy about this.

Tssss… You're a lot braver than me Jane.

Yeah I know! But hey! You're the Lady in the house, Mary you're what's keeping us together Honey. Mary I'm not doing this without you.

Geeeezzz… Jane! Mwah… Okay look, let's just go and do it, but please don't leave my side on the mission.

Mary! I never leave your side Gurl, I love you! Mary I love you kinda about as much if not slightly more than I love my Pimps probing tool. Haa ha…

Haa ha…Yeah you better! Hmm.... Kissss... Hmmm...

[4.17] COMPLETED

Two days later mission completed...

Here you go, Thank you. (The limo pulls away from the dorm hall). Open the door Jane before I collapse. Okay, we're home! Ooooogh! This cum-stained sofa feels sooo good.

Aaaah...I'm soooo tired. What a trip. Unfucking-believable! Oooh! Mary Look there's two bouquets of roses here.

Wow! That's sweet of the Ladies! Read the cards.

To my precious Jane, mission well done. I pray for your recovery my child. Your reward will be what you dream of, hint, hint, every inch of me. Your always grateful Pimp, Cardinal Yaoi.

To my dear Mary, I'm sure you had a safe and pleasurable time in **Kuntfucky** and hope you look forward to many more adventures. Your forever merciful & extremely virile Pimp, Cardinal Rimme.

Pisssss... PUFF, pisssss... PUFF! Whoa! Geeezzz! The cards just went up in smoke! There's nothing but ashes left. Wild, absolutely wild!

Aaaaah! Jane I don't care what goes up in smoke, and screw their pontificating, I'm just so glad to be home.

Yep! We're home and we're safe and nothing happen to us except getting sore screw holes. Mwah... I told you it was safe.

Yeah, Jane, it was just like you said. An in-and-out mission.

Yeah, four hundred penetrations worth of, in-and-outs. I swear my Rose is broken.

Aaah... Baby, don't worry. I'm going to fix your broken Vaganus® later and make it all better. Kiss.... Hmmm.... I love you. Mwah...

It was amazing. Mary you stole the show.

What do you mean?

When we arrived there and we approached the security desk at the entrance, I was so nervous I walked behind you but you just did that proud peacock strut of yours.

What strut?

The, I'm the hottest bitch in the world strut, you know the walk I'm talking about, were the boys just stand there in awe with their mouths open.

Oh, that walk. Haa... ha... Jane, it's just the way I walk, I don't have a, strut.

Anyway, you walked in and the guards were mortified by your stunning beauty and of course they just melted. Your un-freaken-believable seductive powers amaze me! And then the next thing you know they had their horny little dicks out looking to mount our beautiful exposed Rosebuds. They popped their dicks in and then, BOOM! Light out, they hit the floor.

Yeah, but Jane they were the horniness, most gullible, smallest pecker, Non-Stud saps I've ever had the pleasure to take up my cooch! It was more like pity sex. And Jane it was easy peasy just like you said it was gonna be. But answer me this my insatiable little spy-chick? How were you so sure it was gonna be so, easy peasy?

Well Mary, look at it this way, our Pimps, Yaoi and RimMe, I really don't think they want to lose us, and I mean EVER lose us. They treat us like we're precious pieces of gold or something. I just had a feeling they thought the whole thing out very carefully and knew there was no real danger involved. You heard them, when they said,

No harm will ever cum to you

It's like they were having a prophecy, giving us a message from the Cock-God or something. Creepy!

Ha... haa ha.... ha... Yeah, I think you're right, because the guards didn't even carry guns! Jane, they were just a bunch of docile, submissive, pansy peanut sized, Non-Studs. Definitely the guards were weak, effeminate, cowardly type men. It was too easy. Hell I have a feeling maybe our Pimps numbed them up for us before we got there with something in the ventilation system.

Geeeeez! You're right Mare. They weren't violent like most humans. Maybe we could have recruited some of them to Opt-Out and switch their breeding over to Sissies.

Yeah the guards were kind of feminine. I bet they would love to take it up-the-ass! It was all so unreal. I could have knocked them over by blowing on them. And none of their dicks were longer than maybe four inches! I get more pleasure out of a probing wand on a SissySeat® at school or a **Douche-a-Matic®** [4.D-G1.23].

I know Mare, even after they penetrated us and were sedated into a semi-conscious state. They just keep poking at our loveholes like zombies.

Oh Jane, once they penetrated me and were drugged, I had to push some of them out of me and down to the floor, just to make room for the next jerk-off. And some of the little zombified assholes would get up off the floor and try to mount me again. I just started kicking them in the ass with my six inch pumps. Talk about surrealistic. Oh, and I think I missed a couple of times and ended up kicking them in the balls. Oh Cock-God, I felt so bad, but NOT!

Haa... haa... Yeah didn't feel sorry for them much.

And Jane, talk about stealing the show, Thanks for taking all the extra dicks I couldn't handle. You're the best little gangbanging Sissy ever! Geeezzz... Jane, my bottom was sore after sixty-nine penetrations or so. But you just kept taking them. I think you must have taken most of the guards last night! I remember you calling out, NEXT! And there wasn't a hard prick in the place. Then you had the biggest satisfied smile of accomplishment on your face.

Agh! It was fun Mare!

Jane you took so many more penetrations than I did. You're such a talented Whore Baby. You should get an award for what you do with your magic Sissy hole! Hmm... Kisss... Thanks Babe!

Oh Thanks Mary. Mwah... But hey I enjoyed it. Kissss...

Oh Jane! We make such a great Sissy team. I persuade men with my elegance and beauty and you screw them till their balls are empty with your sexy little petite fuck-monkey body. We're the prefect Whore team. Anyway, I hope the gold got to Rome.

[4.18] THE TRUTH

The Gurls confide in one another…

Well on the way back from the mission I heard the pilot talking and she said there wasn't as much gold as was expected, so I guess the Government of the United States Inc. really is broke.

Well after this weekend it doesn't have an ounce of gold left, because we took what the Chinese left behind out of pity.

Hey whatever Jane. We're safe. Our employer is the HCC which is the second largest financial entity in the world, China being largest and most sovereign of all nations.

Jane Honey, I don't care if America's broke. I'm proud to be one regardless of what our government is up to. Sexually speaking it's still the land of the FREE and the home of the BRAVE.

Right Babe. You just keep telling yourself that. It's more like, we're FREE to take as much abuse as is administered to us and we're BRAVE enough to play their stupid little monetary game.

JANE!

What? The games called, bending over and taking it up the ass you stupid little animals. And after hearing the sermon from Rimme about the Money-Whores and the Cock-Whores I'm not so sure ANY of this make sense.

JANE!

And we do it. Like the proud idiot American Sissies we are. I mean after all we're made in the USA Inc. Whoohooo! America First! Make America Great Again!

JANE! Stop it! You know I don't like hearing you talk like that. We don't know what's happening in Washingcum! Donald (the douche-bag) might be the best President ever!

Yeah! Who knows, Re-Pubic-Cunts, Demo-Cunts, it's all one big Corporatocracy anyway. And sure! Of course we're proud American Sissies. If it wasn't for our profiteering Government, us non-impregnable, vagina-substitute creatures wouldn't even exist. After all our government is the, masters of Financial-Sodomy!

JANE! What did I say! Don't let me hear you talking like this way again! I just got elected the new freshman class president. And who knows maybe after college I'll be involved in politics. Especially now with our affiliation with the **NSA**®. It's a powerful political tool Jane. Who knows what might happen. As my life-partner Jane, you can't go around talking stink about the USA Inc. government.

Okay, okay... Geeezzz... (Jane confides). **Mary**, don't blame me! Hey! You know I'm proud to be an American too! And it's not what we are. It's who we're being abused by! I'm only saying **the Truth**. You gotta admit, the USA Inc. government has metaphorically screwed everyone and every Cunt-tree in the ass and this was all at the barrel of a gun. In reality the bankers own the United States Inc. It's clear what's happening!

What's that Sugar-puss?

The USA Inc. government points the gun and the Bankers pull the trigger! And as for the democracy ploy it's,

Bullshit... !!!...

Huh! America the defenders of freedom. Freedom my ass, **Mare**. The United States of America Incorporated is a money-whoring maggot not a democracy. Mare! We're proof of that. Normal people don't raise livestock animals like us to bang em in the ass, physically or financially!

Jane, calm down. You know I'm not naive. And I'm proud like you Baby! But I know our fascist government or business or whatever you wanna call it, here in the United States Inc. this thing they call a Cunt-tree owns both of us. We're the property of the government.

Yeah **Mary**, no kidding and it hasn't improved in hundreds of years. The Federal Reserve and the Holy Cockolic Church Banks, the fascists are the wealthy Stud® bureaucrats. Don't you see? It's all the same! Banker's start wars not governments. Just look at history, it took the US government centuries to figure-out the global reach of its military is just another way of projecting imperialism! It's got NOTHING to do with democracy!

So what are you trying to say Jane? Nothing has changed in United States Inc. It's the same game with a new set of players?

Yeah! The only difference is we tried to control the world with guns and now we're trying to control it with Sissy **Vaganus**®. In other words, us, we're the new cum-modity! The Sissy is the export product and Sissydom® is the new American geopolitical policy. Let's face it, the greed for money is America's down fall as was every empire before it.

Jane, yes I know and agree with all of it my Lover! Mwah… Its BIG Pharma, BIG military, BIG business and BIG banks. They own this screwed up Cunt-tree, now and in the past. In the UA Inc., me and you Jane, we're just players in the game, we're pawns, breed for profit herd animals.

After all these years, the United States is still a screwed-up imperialistic war machine. And if you believe your cute little twink looking body and your Sissy Vaganus® is a replacement for a vagina, well then you're as screwed-up as they are!

Yep! I'm a vagina replacement Whore.

Look Jane, I know the whole thing, with the MSES, Sissy-Stud class inequality, the new US Second **Cunt-Stitution** [17], Sissy-Sex as labor compensation. To me it's all one big bullshit story. And I'm not an idiot Jane. I just go along with all the propaganda produced so I can profit for the both of us.

I know **Mare**. Sorry, I get all upset about the disparity, lack of hope and the generally disingenuous government.

Hey I don't care Honey-Puss if this means having a government job, working as a Hoe or be cuming a cum-guzzling Money-Whore of a politician in Washingcum DC! I'll do it! If it means the two of us being happy together. **Jane** from the bottom of my heart, I'll do whatever it takes to make you happy. Huh! (hugs) this is how much you mean to me Jane.... kisss.... Mwah...

Mwah... Oh Mare, I love you so much. If you're elected to a government position in Washingcum I want to be your office Whore. I'll do anybody you want me to. I'll do anything to make you more powerful because I know this is what my DOM wants and needs!

Haaa.... haa.... Okay you promiscuous little Bitch of mine. Ooooh! Wow! Ahhhh... All this talk about power and gold made my Cocklette squirt a load in my panties. Aghhhh... And makes me think about the HCC and Rome and Pimps and.... Ooooh! I squirted again... Aghhh...My heads spinning.

Ooooh! Me too Baby. Geeezzz... I wonder if we'll ever get to meet her.

Who?

The Holy **Cock-Pope** [9.I3.7] in the Vaticum! She must be awesome to have sex with.

Well someday maybe we'll have a chance. They say Italy's beautiful.

Like me Lover?

Yes, like you, my Sissy-Gurl. Hmmm... Kisss.... As beautiful as you! My dear sweet Jane. Mwah...

Hey they say her prick is two feet long and she has the biggest one in the world!

Yeah, Jane you continually remind me of this. Thanks. Haaa.... haa... ha... Oh Jane Honey, I love you sooo much... kisss. Mwah...

Mary I love you too Lady. Kiss.... Kisss.... Mwah...

Jane! We're gonna have so many wonderful adventures together! This is just the beginning! Hmmm.... Kiss.... Kisssss.... Mwah... Mwah...

Continued in EN04, Chapter 1....

=== THE END ===

Review Request & Suggestion

Thanks for purchasing this book or bundle (four book set). Please leave a review on Google Books, Amazon or Audible. Also to help our readers or listeners, we strongly suggest downloading the Empty Nation manual **SM069** to assist with the complexity of the story from any one of the following.

Audible.com, free after purchase as a Product Summary

Amazon.com, (low price) ASIN: 1719912866

Google Play Books, (free) GGKEY: X02BGY24G4K

The Official Sissydom Manual SM069

The National Sissydom Association (NSA)
A subsidiary of USA Inc.
All rights reserved, copyright 2018
Revised: 11-01-2018

SM069-03 Description

The Sissydom® manual version SM069-03 encompasses details from years 2213 to 2251. This manual is intended to be used by United States Inc. citizens for the sole purpose of clarification of the procedures, laws, rule, codes, regulations, probing, documents, exams, rating, ranking, classification, drugs, qualifications and behavior of all parties participating or remotely involved in the United States Inc. MSES (US-MSES).

TERRITORIES

This manual also applies to all occupied territories under control of the USA Inc. Including but not limited to all of Latin America (LA) including countries in both Central & South America; refer to the LA-MSES.

SAR

Special Administrative Regions (SARs) enjoy a higher degree of autonomy under the "one Cock, one Cunt" concept developed by President Tramp. There are currently two SARs, Mexico located in the Central America and Canada in North America. Both were turned over to USA Inc. control after the NAFTA War in 2169. Both SARs mentioned here implement the LCT system.

Persons living in a SAR are NOT and never will be citizens of the USA Inc. Also neither is allowed to cross into the USA Inc. at any time (visas are not available) unless the border-crossing is for a female surrendering her rights and becomes a host-mother at a Sissy Farm Breeding facility.

MSES AFFILIATES

Although the following Cunt-Trees are not controlled territories or SARs of the USA Inc. they are dependent and liable to the USA Inc. monetarily. This pretty much means, the USA Inc. can squeeze their balls at any time to induce compliance.

IN-MSES (India)
RU-MSES (Russia)
IS-MSES (Islamic)
AU-MSES (Africa Union)
SE-MSES (Southeast Asia)

These Cunt-Trees are all implementing the MSES LCT system of payment (aka the new SWIFT system). For local rules and regulations consult the specific sections in this manual (section not available yet).

RULES

The rules and laws stated in this document are lawful and can be used in a court of law to defend and protect only the rights of United States of America Incorporated citizens. The USA Inc. governing body (Government) and any and all of its proxies or entities, owned, contained, endowed, funded, imprisoned, underwritten, confiscated, authorized, financed, detained, sanctioned, annexed, blockchained, begotten, empowered, captured, incorporated, forfeited, convicted, subjugated, forsaken, subsidized, sponsored, abandoned, franchised, promoted, controlled, conquered, incarcerated, entitled or restrained by said Government or its affiliated corporate members are fully relieved of any and all liability of wrong doing created by adhering to the laws, rules and regulations stated here in this SM069-03 document. Amen.

Please download the current manual for further details in the EN Series…

About the Author Sue Yan Nish

Empty Nation Series published by What Is It Press. As far as the author of the series is concerned, we know very little about the Sue Yan Nish. We think she is a Chinese-American and lives somewhere in China. And although her location changes frequently, we receive cryptic messages form her. The messages simply tell us only that the manuscript is finished and where we need to retrieve it from. We leave her compensation in a small box and in the same place the manuscript was left for us.

Author Contact Info

The following addresses are ways to get in touch with the author Sue Yan Nish.

Author Bio:
https://www.amazon.com/Sue-Yan Nish/e/B07GW252V1

Emails:
sueyannish@outlook.com
sueyannish@gmail.com

Website:
https://sites.google.com/view/empty-nation/home

www.ingramcontent.com/pod-product-compliance
Lightning Source LLC
Chambersburg PA
CBHW031305120626
46554CB00001BA/296